# THE EDENBOURG TATTLER

## March 2001

Word has it
that with the king's disappearance
**Princess Dominique Stanbury**
has returned to Edenbourg sporting a
green complexion and enough bouts of
morning sickness to draw some very
serious conclusions. Not only that, but
**Marcus Kent**, the king's right-hand man,
hasn't left her side since she
stepped off the royal jet. Could it be
that Marcus is responsible for the
princess's *delicate* condition? And if the
king is ever found, will he condone
Marcus's inclusion in the royal mix and
allow his loyal employee to marry the
princess he's so obviously in love with?

\* \* \* \* \* \*

*Check out next month's*
*The Blacksheep Prince's Bride*
*(SR #1510)*
*by Martha Shields*
*to find out what happens!*

Dear Reader,

You asked for more ROYALLY WED titles and you've got them! For the next four months we've brought back the Stanbury family—first introduced in a short story by Carla Cassidy on our eHarlequin.com Web site. Be sure to check the archives to find Nicholas's story! But don't forget to pick up Stella Bagwell's *The Expectant Princess* and discover the involving story of the disappearance of King Michael.

Other treats this month include Marie Ferrarella's one hundredth title for Silhouette Books! This wonderful, charming and emotional writer shows her trademark warmth and humor in *Rough Around the Edges*. Luckily for all her devoted readers, Marie has at least another hundred plots bubbling in her imagination, and we'll be seeing more from her in many of our Silhouette lines.

Then we've got Karen Rose Smith's *Tall, Dark & True* about a strong, silent sheriff who can't bear to keep quiet about his feelings any longer. And Donna Clayton's heroine asks *Who Will Father My Baby?*—and gets a surprising answer. *No Place Like Home* by Robin Nicholas is a delightful read that reminds us of an all-time favorite movie—I'll let you guess which one! And don't forget first-time author Roxann Delaney's debut title, *Rachel's Rescuer*.

Next month be sure to return for *The Blacksheep Prince's Bride* by Martha Shields, the next of the ROYALLY WED series. Also returning are popular authors Judy Christenberry and Elizabeth August.

Happy reading!

*Mary-Theresa Hussey*

Mary-Theresa Hussey
Senior Editor

---

Please address questions and book requests to:
Silhouette Reader Service
U.S.: 3010 Walden Ave., P.O. Box 1325, Buffalo, NY 14269
Canadian: P.O. Box 609, Fort Erie, Ont. L2A 5X3

# The
# Expectant Princess

## STELLA BAGWELL

SILHOUETTE *Romance*®

Published by Silhouette Books

America's Publisher of Contemporary Romance

Special thanks and acknowledgment are given to
Stella Bagwell for her contribution
to the ROYALLY WED: THE STANBURYS series.

To Lloyd Henry Cook, who was surely a king in a past life,
or at the very least a prince. This one is for you, dear brother.

 SILHOUETTE BOOKS

ISBN 0-373-19504-4

THE EXPECTANT PRINCESS

## Books by Stella Bagwell

### Silhouette Romance

*Golden Glory* #469
*Moonlight Bandit* #485
*A Mist on the Mountain* #510
*Madeline's Song* #543
*The Outsider* #560
*The New Kid in Town* #587
*Cactus Rose* #621
*Hillbilly Heart* #634
*Teach Me* #657
*The White Night* #674
*No Horsing Around* #699
*That Southern Touch* #723
*Gentle as a Lamb* #748
*A Practical Man* #789
*Precious Pretender* #812
*Done to Perfection* #836
*Rodeo Rider* #878
*\*Their First Thanksgiving* #903
*\*The Best Christmas Ever* #909

*\*New Year's Baby* #915
*Hero in Disguise* #954
*Corporate Cowgirl* #991
*Daniel's Daddy* #1020
*A Cowboy for Christmas* #1052
*Daddy Lessons* #1085
*Wanted: Wife* #1140
*†The Sheriff's Son* #1218
*†The Rancher's Bride* #1224
*†The Tycoon's Tots* #1228
*†The Rancher's Blessed*
*Event* #1296
*†The Ranger and the Widow*
*Woman* #1314
*†The Cowboy and the Debutante* #1334
*†Millionaire on Her Doorstep* #1368
*The Bridal Bargain* #1414
*Falling for Grace* #1456
*The Expectant Princess* #1504

### Silhouette Special Edition

*Found: One Runaway Bride* #1049
*†Penny Parker's Pregnant!* #1258

### Silhouette Books

Fortunes of Texas
*The Heiress and the Sheriff*

Maitland Maternity
*Just for Christmas*

\*Heartland Holidays
†Twins on the Doorstep

## STELLA BAGWELL

sold her first book to Silhouette in 1985. More than forty novels later, she still says she isn't completely content unless she's writing. Recently she and her husband of thirty years moved from the hills of Oklahoma to Seadrift, Texas. Stella says the water, the tropical climate and the seabirds make it a lovely place to let her imagination soar.

She and her husband have one son, Jason, who lives and teaches high school math in nearby Port Lavaca.

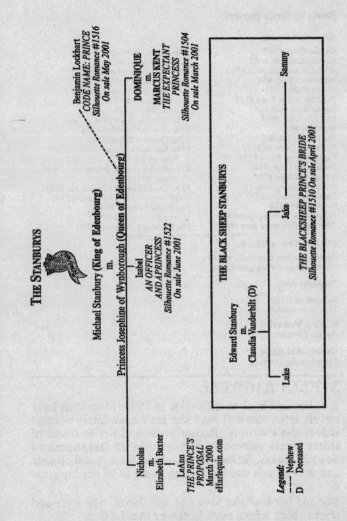

# THE STANBURYS

Benjamin Lockhart
*CODE NAME: PRINCE*
Silhouette Romance #1516
On sale May 2001

Michael Stanbury (King of Edenbourg)
m.
Princess Josephine of Wynborough (Queen of Edenbourg)

DOMINIQUE
m.
MARCUS KENT
*THE EXPECTANT PRINCESS*
Silhouette Romance #1504
On sale March 2001

Isabel
*AN OFFICER AND A PRINCESS*
Silhouette Romance #1522
On sale June 2001

Nicholas
m.
Elizabeth Baxter

LeAnn
*THE PRINCE'S PROPOSAL*
March 2000
eHarlequin.com

## THE BLACK SHEEP STANBURYS

Edward Stanbury
m.
Claudia Vanderbilt (D)

Luke        Jake        Sammy

*THE BLACKSHEEP PRINCE'S BRIDE*
Silhouette Romance #1510 On sale April 2001

**Legend:**
--- Nephew
D  Deceased

# *Prologue*

*March, 2001*

"She's going to be a beautiful princess."

Queen Josephine of Edenbourg's announcement was accompanied with a tender smile for the three-month-old baby cradled in the arms of her doting father.

"LeAnn already *is* a beautiful princess," Prince Nicholas proudly corrected his mother. "She's going to grow up to be the spitting image of Rebecca."

The prince's comment produced a blush on the face of his young American-born wife and happy laughter among the group crowded around the baby and her proud parents.

Outside, a cool rain was falling on the majestic towers of Edenbourg Abbey, but inside the ancient cathedral the mood was warm and festive. Family, friends and dignitaries from several countries had gathered to attend the christening of baby LeAnn, first grandchild of the king and queen of Edenbourg, one of the most beautiful countries in Eastern Europe, and daughter to the heir to the throne.

"Well put, my son. LeAnn *is* already quite beautiful," Josephine agreed. The slender woman with a sleek brown chignon and regal stature touched a gentle finger to the baby's rosy cheek. "And so far she's behaved like a little angel."

"Yes, so far," Rebecca spoke up in worried motherly fashion. "But I fear once the bishop takes hold of her she's going to start wailing at the top of her lungs."

Once more chuckles abounded throughout the group. As if on cue, the baby looked around with wide innocent eyes, then not caring one whit that her audience was made up of royal bloodlines dating back to medieval times, she gave them a toothless grin.

Standing at the prince's right elbow, golden-haired Princess Dominique Stanbury, the youngest of the Stanbury siblings, smiled affectionately as she reached for her new niece.

"Let me hold her, dear brother. You're positively too greedy where your daughter is concerned. You're going to have her spoiled rotten before she's old enough to sit upright."

With a groan of feigned reluctance, the tall young prince with black hair handed the baby to his younger sister. "That's what princesses are for, aren't they? To be spoiled. Father certainly pampered you," he teased.

A spate of laughter followed his words. Dominique wrinkled her nose at him and glanced at her older sister, Isabel, who was standing a few steps away from their brother. "Isabel, you're not going to let him get away with that, are you?"

Princess Isabel laughed as her gaze seesawed back and forth between her two siblings. Like Dominique, she possessed a tall, slender build and light green eyes. But where Dominique's thick mane was golden brown and fell to the middle of her back, Isabel's was dark brown and just brushed the top of her shoulders. An impish smile appeared on her face as she spoke. "Don't worry, sister, LeAnn will give our brother a special lesson in spoiling princesses. And I can't wait to see how well he holds up under the strain."

The whole family chuckled, except for little LeAnn. The baby began to fuss and Dominique instinctively rocked her with a gentle swaying motion. At the same time, she noticed her mother's attention was once again riveted to her wristwatch. The gesture was out of character for Josephine, who approached every social event with smooth and steady confidence.

Bending her head toward her mother's ear, she asked, "What's wrong, Mother? You've been checking the time after every minute."

Casting an anxious eye toward the massive carved doors at the entrance of the cathedral, the queen said, "It's really getting rather late in the hour. I expected your father to be here by now."

Catching the last part of his mother's distressed comment, Nicholas consulted the timepiece strapped to his wrist. "There's still fifteen minutes before the ceremony starts. I'm sure Father will be showing up any minute."

Exasperation was evident in the brief shake of Josephine's head. "I tried to persuade him to ride with me this morning, but he insisted he had some sort of brief business to take care of before he joined us here at the abbey. He then left with only an armed driver. I do hope there hasn't been some sort of trouble that forced him to return to the castle."

The queen turned a commanding look on her son.

"Nicholas, go question security. Perhaps they've been in radio contact."

As the prince walked away to do her bidding, Dominique pulled her mother a few steps aside of the group of family and friends.

"It isn't like you to get so alarmed, Mother," she said in a hushed tone. "I'm sure Father was just detained with business. It certainly won't be the first time."

Queen Josephine gave her daughter a halfhearted smile. "You are right. But something—" With another unusual display of nerves, she pressed a jeweled hand to her throat. "I can't explain it. But something has left me with an uneasy feeling. Michael was so looking forward to his granddaughter's christening and—"

Her words paused as the guests around them began to exchange excited whispers and stare toward the entrance of the cathedral.

Both mother and daughter turned to see the line of security at the massive doors had parted and a tall man with gray hair was striding toward the congregation standing near the altar. A younger, dark-haired man followed immediately on his heels.

The massive size of the church made the distance too great to exactly identify the men. But from the tall stature and gray hair of the older one, Dominique was certain it had to be her father, the king.

She turned a relieved smile on her mother. "See, there he is now. Your worrying was all for naught."

A slight frown creased Josephine's forehead as she continued to study the advancing male figures. "That isn't Michael. I don't recognize either of these men."

By now Nicholas had returned from questioning the guards. His grim expression caused such alarm to rush through Dominique, she completely forgot about the two strangers.

"What does security say?" Josephine quickly questioned him.

Nicholas shook his head. "They haven't heard from Father since he and his driver left the castle more than an hour ago. A detail is out checking the route at this very moment."

Before mother or sister could question him further, the two unknown men, accompanied by one security guard, approached the queen.

All went suddenly quiet and everyone in the huge church looked on with a bit of amazement as the elder of the two men bowed deeply from the waist. A royal christening with gate-crashers didn't happen in Edenbourg. Not even rarely.

In a voice loud enough for everyone to hear, he said, "Your Majesty, I hope you will forgive me for trespassing on this special occasion. I am your husband's brother, Edward Stanbury. And this is my eldest son, Luke." He gestured toward the younger man at his side, who in turn bowed to the queen.

Murmurs of disbelief rippled through the guests while Josephine simply stared at the two intruders. From the rigid line of her jaw, Dominique could tell her mother was trying not to reveal her shock at this sudden turn of events. Edward Stanbury had left the country of Edenbourg years ago to become a citizen of the United States. He and King Michael were estranged and had been for as long as Dominique could remember.

"You've traveled far," Josephine finally spoke to the two men. "Does King Michael know of your arrival?"

Edward opened his mouth to answer, but before he could utter a word, his son, Luke, quickly interceded.

"We've only just now come from the airport, Your Majesty, and—"

The remainder of the younger man's sentence was missed as another flurry of activity caused everyone's attention to swing once again to the entrance of the cathedral. Instantly, mouths gaped and soft gasps of alarm sounded. A royal guard was rushing toward the christening party as if demons were on his heels.

Clearly anticipating that something was amiss, Nicholas put a bracing hand under his mother's elbow. Next to Dominique, Rebecca silently reached for her daughter. Dominique carefully handed LeAnn back to her sister-in-law and waited with the rest as the young guard bowed before the royal family.

"What is it, man?" Nicholas demanded impatiently.

The guard's words came out in a breathless rush. "I fear it's bad news, Your Highness. The king and his driver have been involved in an accident. The car crashed through a guardrail and careened down the side of a steep cliff. We believe both men are dead."

Wails of utter shock and horror rose from the crowd to echo off the hallowed walls of the cathedral. Before Dominique could begin to comprehend the news, a security detail was surrounding Nicholas.

At the same time, Marcus Kent, the king's high counsel, was pushing his way forward through the group of stunned dignitaries and friends.

In a daze, Dominique watched as he lay his hand on her brother's shoulder and soberly spoke, "According to the Edenbourg Treatise, it is now my solemn duty to proclaim Nicholas to be the acting king of Edenbourg until Michael is found or declared dead."

Josephine gripped her son's arm. "What do you

mean found?'' she asked Marcus. ''Has the king's body not yet been recovered?''

Marcus shook his head. ''No. Security has just now informed me that King Michael's body is missing from the accident scene.''

Dominique didn't hear the laments of those around her. Nor did she realize a cry of pain was spilling from her own lips as she pressed a hand to her stomach and rushed from the abbey.

## Chapter One

A few steps away from the cathedral's grassy court-yard, Dominique laid her cheek against a column of cool marble and tried to calm her roiling stomach.

Dear God, don't let me be sick now, she silently prayed. Her mother, her family were going to need her strength. They couldn't be burdened with the secret she carried. At least, not now.

Even though she desperately tried to hold them back, tears poured from her eyes. She was a princess, bred and tutored to be strong under the very worst of cir-cumstances. If her father knew she was displaying such emotion in a public place he would be horrified and angry.

The sobering thought braced her somewhat and she forced herself to dig a tiny embroidered kerchief from her handbag. With trembling hands, she carefully dabbed at the moisture beneath her eyes.

"Dominique? Are you all right?"

Dominique's heart went still, then lurched into a

hard, anxious thud. Nearly four years had passed since she'd seen him, but the male voice behind her was as familiar as yesterday's sunset.

Squaring her shoulders, she stepped away from the marble column and turned to face the man she'd tried her best to forget.

Even before Marcus Kent had become her father's top adviser, he'd been an impressive figure of a man both intellectually and physically. At two inches over six feet, he was all lean muscle and broad shoulders. Short, raven-black hair waved slightly back from a wide forehead and strong, roughly chiseled features. Thick black eyebrows and lashes framed a pair of eyes that were nothing less than striking. Their smoky-topaz color was as unique as the man himself.

At thirty-three he was twelve years Dominique's senior. Yet as she gazed at him now, she knew she had never met a man who stirred her more.

"It wasn't necessary for you to check on me, Marcus. But thank you just the same."

Three strides carried him to within inches of her and she felt herself quivering with renewed awareness as his solemn gaze searched her upturned face. The years she'd been away at university in the States had been kind to him. He looked just as virile and potently masculine as he had that day she'd said goodbye.

"You were very white when you fled your family a moment ago. I wanted to make certain you hadn't fainted."

"I'm sure a guard followed me." She wouldn't know of life any other way. Being a member of a royal family made her a target. She'd long ago had to counsel herself to the fact that her movements in public, no matter how trivial, were almost always watched and her behavior scrutinized. Especially here in the city of Old Stanbury.

"I expect at this moment you need more than a guard's presence."

His gentle suggestion caused pricks of fresh tears to burn the backs of her eyes. Determined to do her father proud, she blinked and sniffed and swallowed them down. But the idea that King Michael might really be gone from their lives drained the very strength from her legs and she grabbed for Marcus's hand almost at the same moment he reached out to steady her.

"Oh, Marcus," she said hoarsely. "This has to be a nightmare. Please tell me Father can't be dead."

From the moment Marcus had spotted Dominique entering the cathedral this morning, his insides had gathered into hard knots and remained that way. In the past few days, he'd learned from the king himself that she was home from university to attend this morning's christening. But he'd deliberately avoided going by her suite of rooms in the family's palace to say hello.

Years ago Marcus had made a point to quell her schoolgirl adulation for him and, in doing so, he suspected he'd crushed her young pride. At the time he'd not set out to deliberately hurt or embarrass her. Quite the opposite, in fact. He'd always been genuinely fond of Dominique and he'd wanted to send her off to university with a clear mind. Not cluttered with romantic notions for an older man.

Four years had passed since then, and he figured somewhere in between she'd forgiven him for forcing her to take off her rose-colored glasses where he was concerned. As for himself, the years Dominique had been away had seen him married with high hopes, then divorced with bitter regret.

Now he wished he had made a point of seeing Dominique before this morning. Maybe then he would have been prepared for the drastic change in her appearance. She'd grown into a woman whose beauty knocked the very breath from his lungs.

Her tall, slender body now moved with grace and poise. The golden-brown cap of curls he remembered framing her face had grown into long waves that very nearly touched the back of her waist. Today the thick tresses were pulled back from her temples with diamond-studded combs that matched the loops of diamonds dangling from her earlobes. He recalled her eyes being the same pale green he was looking into, only now their open innocence was gone, replaced by a provocative slant and a touch of shadowy mystery that was utterly feminine. A perfectly straight nose led down to an equally perfect set of lips. Plump and moist; the top lip dipped deeply in the middle, the bottom curved to an enticing pout.

No doubt she had been properly kissed since he'd last seen her, Marcus thought. In fact, for all he knew, she might have already given her heart to some young man.

The gentle pressure of her fingers tightening around his brought Marcus out of his wandering thoughts—thoughts that were both foolish and improper on his part. It didn't matter that her cream-colored dress did more than hint at the luscious curves of a woman. To him she could be nothing more than the king's young daughter. A king who, it appeared, was most likely dead.

"I'm sorry, Dominique. I can't give you hope when there seems to be none."

Her head dropped, then swung from side to side in

disbelief. The sudden urge to pull her into his arms and comfort her shocked Marcus. Although he didn't know why his feelings should be a surprise to him. Where Dominique was concerned, he'd always harbored a protective streak. Six years ago, when he'd joined the king's administrative staff, she'd been a shy, gangly fifteen-year-old. Uncertain of her place in the royal family and at the same time hungry for reassurance and affection. His own rough childhood had helped to create an affinity for the young princess. One that obviously hadn't dissolved, in spite of the past years she'd been away.

"What about LeAnn's christening?" she murmured. "Are they still going through with the ceremony?"

"No," he answered, his thoughts softening his voice. "The accident has taken precedence now. Your family is making preparations to return to the castle."

Her head came up swiftly. "Oh. Then I must get back inside."

With her free hand she pressed the kerchief against both cheeks, then snapped the dainty cloth away in the small gold velvet bag hanging from her shoulder.

Marcus released her hand, then cupped his palm around her bent elbow. As he guided her through a back entry of the cathedral, he wished above anything that she didn't have to face the sorrow of her father's accident. He wished it was in his power to shield her now and always from life's harsh realities.

But he was just a man. A commoner, despite his lofty position as the king's high counsel. She deserved and needed more than he could ever give her and he suspected she'd learned that while she'd been away, growing into a woman.

* * *

Three days later Dominique was still struggling to shake the notion that her father's horrific accident was all just a nightmare. Each morning she expected to wake and join her family in the dining hall for breakfast. Somehow she knew she would find King Michael seated at the head of the long table, a cup of tea in one hand, a newspaper in the other. But each morning she'd discovered the dining hall empty, her mother choosing to breakfast in privacy, while her brother, Nicholas, was already at work, trying to deal with the upheaval their father's disappearance had caused with the media and the political world.

This morning Dominique had chosen to breakfast on the balcony off her bedroom. If she were going to eat alone, at least she could do it in total solitude without a bevy of servants hovering over her.

Being away at university had spoiled her, she supposed. While living on campus and attending classes, she'd not been smothered by a royal entourage to carry out even her smallest bidding. Over time, she'd grown to love the freedom, the feeling that basically she was no different than any other young woman working toward a degree. Even if she was Princess Dominique Stanbury of Edenbourg.

The slight sound of a footstep on flagstone alerted her that she was no longer alone. Glancing up from a plate of fruit, she saw that Prudence, her lady-in-waiting, had joined her on the balcony.

Only two years older than herself, Prudence had been with Dominique since their early childhood. When the time had come for Dominique to go to college, Prudence had begged to go along with her princess, but the king and queen had separated the two, believing it would help their daughter develop more independence. Now that Dominique was back, Prudence was delighted and had practically been smothering her with attention.

At the moment, the young woman with dark brown hair twisted into an elaborate coil at the back of her head gave her princess a rueful smile. "I'm sorry to disturb you, Dominique. But someone has asked to see you. Are you feeling up to a visitor this morning?"

"Who is it, Pru?"

The other woman's smile deepened. "Marcus Kent. I thought you might not want me to send him away."

Other than a faint lift of her eyebrows, Dominique made no reply to her lady's subtle hint. Instead, she glanced down at her blue velour robe. She wasn't properly dressed, but she was decently covered. And Marcus might have received some sort of news about her father that he wanted to deliver personally.

"I'll see him here on the balcony. Oh, and Pru," she added as her personal attendant turned to hurry away. "Please send a servant up with a pot of fresh decaffeinated coffee and a thermos of cold fruit juice. Mr. Kent might want refreshments."

"Of course," she said with a wide smile. "I'll be in the study if you need me for anything else."

Prudence disappeared back into the palace and Dominique quickly finger-combed her loose hair. Thankfully, she had taken the time to thoroughly brush the long strands before breakfast. But without combs or headbands to confine it, the waves slipped and slid to their choosing rather than hers.

Oh, what did it matter anyway, she thought dismally. Most likely Marcus still thought of her as a young schoolgirl. No doubt he probably believed the crush she'd had on him for a while had died since her time away at university. It didn't matter that she looked less than her best.

The thought was hardly out of her head when a tall shadow appeared across the glass tabletop. Looking up, she squinted against the bright morning sun streaming around his silhouette.

"Prudence didn't tell me you were still having breakfast," he said in that deep voice she remembered so well. "I should have waited until a later hour to see you."

Shaking her head, Dominique motioned for him to take the chair opposite her.

"You're not interrupting anything. I think I've forced down three bites in the past half hour."

He frowned with disapproval. "That's hardly the way to start your day."

The sight of his dark handsome face had already fed her more than the food on her plate, she realized with sudden shock. Then quickly pushing the unbidden thought away, she said, "I'm not sure when my days start and end now, Marcus. Since the morning of the accident, everything has seemed surreal."

Settling back in the wrought-iron chair, he propped his ankle against his knee. Dominique's gaze slid discreetly over the light gray suit that was perfectly cut to fit his broad shoulders, then on to the strip of pale pink shirt against his tanned neck and the burgundy striped tie lying against his chest. From what she knew of Marcus, his looks or clothing were not that important to him. Seeing to the needs of his king and his country were always first and foremost. Yet he was a man who could throw on an old rugby shirt and a pair of jeans and still manage to look impressive.

Watch it, Dominique, she silently scolded herself. As

a teenager, she'd allowed the image of Marcus Kent to put stars in her eyes. But she was a grown woman now and he was a man who would never see her as anything more than a friend or princess. He'd made that clear years ago. And besides, she'd already made a fool out of herself over one man. There was no way she was going to make a second mistake.

"I've been meaning to stop by and—offer my condolences before now," he said. "But as you might guess, things have been hectic with the ongoing investigation of the accident and getting Nicholas settled in as the new acting king."

Dominique latched on to one word and quickly tossed it back at him. "Condolences? Does that mean—" She swallowed as her throat threatened to close around the words. "Has Father's body been found?"

Shaking his head he started to speak, then stopped abruptly as a maid, dressed in a gray-and-white uniform and carrying a loaded ornate silver tray, appeared on the balcony.

After depositing the tray on the table, the plump older woman stood waiting to serve them. Dominique quickly dismissed her, saying, "Thank you, I'll do it."

With a quick curtsy she left them, and Dominique looked at Marcus. "Would you like coffee or juice?"

"Coffee. With a dollop of cream. No sugar."

She reached for a cup and saucer. The thin, gold-encrusted china rattled loudly in her shaking hands.

Quickly, Marcus leaned forward and took the dishes from her. "Here, let me," he said gently. "You're in no shape to be handling hot liquid."

"I'm sorry, Marcus," she apologized as she watched him pour the coffee. "I guess my nerves are a little frayed."

His smile was indulgent. "I would hate to think of you not being upset at a time like this."

She was a mess. A total mess. And Marcus was the one person she'd always wanted to impress with inner strength and dignity. Instead, she seemed to break down with emotion at the very sight of him. Her behavior toward him made no sense at all.

He lifted a second cup in question and she nodded for answer. After he'd filled it and passed it to her, she said, "Getting back to the accident, just what have you discovered? Anything new?"

Carefully, he sipped the hot coffee, then lowered the wafer-thin cup to its saucer. An odd mixture of apprehension and attraction shot through Dominique as his golden-brown eyes settled on her face.

"You are aware that the police have been combing the cliffs where the accident took place and also searching the sea below?" he asked.

She nodded stiffly. "The television news and all the newspapers have been full of pictures and theories as to what might have occurred the day of the crash. But none of it means much. Nothing will—until my father and his driver are found."

He studied her for a moment longer and Dominique got the impression he was trying to decide whether she was strong enough for any sort of revelation. The idea knotted her already queasy stomach.

"A call from the police came in less than an hour ago. They're still trying to extricate the driver's body from the car. Apparently the metal—at least what was left after the fire—was a mangled mess. And I'm sure they're going slowly so as not to destroy any clues. Apparent or otherwise."

Dominique sucked in a fearful breath. "What about my father? If the driver—"

Marcus lifted one hand to halt her tortured thoughts. "King Michael's body has still not been found. The chief investigator believes he must have been tossed from the car, and from that point his body rolled down the cliff and into the sea. The next step is to bring in divers and search the waters just off the island."

Dominique shuddered with imagined horror. "But wouldn't the body have already washed up to the shoreline? The prevailing winds over the North Sea would push the tide toward us, not away."

"That's true, however—"

She darted a questioning frown at him. "But what? What are you not telling me?"

His gaze dropped to her slender fingers and the cup lightly clutched in their grasp. She was so soft and vulnerable. He wanted to shield her from the awful truth and the pain it was bound to bring her.

"Drink your coffee," he suggested quietly.

Her frown deepened, drawing her delicate eyebrows together to create one thin slash above her eyes. "Don't stall, Marcus. Tell me what else you're thinking."

His lips formed a grim line, then he sighed. "You don't really want to think of all the hazards out in the sea."

The stiffness went out of her shoulders and her whole upper body sagged forward with reluctant defeat.

"You mean sharks," she said in a low, raw voice. "Well, you are right. A body wouldn't last long once a scavenger found it. But Father might not have been dead. He might have been dazed and hurt." Her tone suddenly took on a fresh burst of hope. "It's possible he could have wandered off before anyone came upon the wreckage!''

Thoughtfully, Marcus rubbed a thumb along the slight cleft in his chin. "Possible. But not likely. Eventually he would have had to stagger onto someone. There isn't a soul in this city who wouldn't recognize King Michael and carry him to the hospital.''

Although the weather was sunny with only a gentle breeze to ruffle the earliest spring leaves, Dominique felt suddenly cold. Clutching the lapels of her robe tightly together, she said, "Unless he happened to stumble onto an enemy.''

Marcus stared at her in disbelief.

She asked, "Why are you looking at me like that? I realize Father was a beloved king, but one never knows about people anymore. There are some strange ones out there.''

Actually the same sort of thread had run through his own thoughts these past three days. But he'd not voiced it to anyone. Even the police. Not that they would have put any credence into his theory. He was a political adviser, not a detective. And anyway, it was a farfetched notion. Anyone who looked at the scene of the accident would think it incredible for anyone to survive.

"I'm sorry if I was staring, Dominique. Your thoughts just took me by surprise. I didn't expect you to be thinking in such—sinister terms.''

With a shake of her head, she placed her cup back on its saucer. Her fingers trembled as she passed them over her forehead. "I'm not sure I'm thinking at all right now, Marcus. I keep telling myself I have to accept that my father is dead. But my heart refuses. I can't let go of the hope that he still might be alive and out there somewhere—someplace where he can't get back to us.''

Before Marcus realized what he was doing, he reached over and gathered her hand in his.

"You need to put this out of your mind as best you can, Dominique. Fretting about it won't accomplish anything. And you've only just now come back home to the palace. Why don't you see old friends and try to enjoy being with your family."

The warm strength of his hand felt far too good. It was all she could do to keep from turning her palm upward and sliding her fingers intimately between his.

*Oh my, you are a little fool, Dominique. You were supposed to have forgotten all about Marcus Kent. You were certain you had. But you come home and he gives you one kind look and you melt like sweet chocolate between warm lips.*

Clearing her throat, she said, "I'm not going back to my studies anytime soon, Marcus. At least not until this thing with my father is cleared up."

She couldn't tell him that her father's accident was only part of the reason she was delaying her return to university. He'd want a full explanation and she couldn't give him one. The reason would come out all too soon anyway. And then he'd be looking at her with disgust. As no doubt her family would be, too.

# Chapter Two

"Do you think that's a wise decision? Not going back to the university right away?" Marcus asked.

A wan smile tilted Dominique's lips. "I've been known to make unwise choices before. You know me, I never had the level head my sister Isabel possesses. Nor Nicholas's intelligence. But even if this thing with father wasn't happening, I need some time off. To rest."

His smile held a hint of both censure and understanding. "I suppose you'll get to that degree soon enough. And then you'll be out in the world of high-powered business."

Because the pleasure was becoming too great, she slid her hand from his and reached for her coffee. After a thoughtful sip, she said, "I've changed the direction of my degree sometime back. I'm going into the field of education."

His eyebrows lifted. "Oh. I had the impression you wanted to be a financial adviser."

She grimaced. "I've decided it's more important for

a person to acquire an education. Without that, they won't need a financial adviser.'' Shrugging, she self-consciously glanced away from him. ''Eventually I would like to form an education center here in Old Stanbury. For needy students who can't afford to attend private schools or expensive universities.''

''That's a lofty goal,'' he said.

Yes, she thought. And to achieve such a project she was going to need the backing of her family and country. But once her secret was out, Dominique wasn't sure she would receive either. She would probably be lucky if her family didn't choose to disown her completely. While she'd been away at her studies, she'd not behaved as a princess representing her country. But, dear heaven, she was only human, she reasoned with herself. She was a young woman with needs just like thousands of other women in Edenbourg.

Her fidgeting fingers on the cup handle didn't go unnoticed by Marcus. In fact, it amazed him that everything about her caught his attention.

In the open light of the fresh morning, her skin looked like rich cream and pale roses. Her brown hair was threaded with streaks of gold and sunlight. This morning the mass was unconfined, the waves tumbling about her face and shoulders like a wild waterfall.

Before Marcus realized where his thinking was headed, he was suddenly wondering what it would be like to run his hands through the thick brown tresses, to skim the pads of his fingers over the smooth skin of her face, her throat and down the shadowy cleavage between her breasts.

Dear Lord, he must be drunk from lack of sleep and too much work, he reasoned with himself. There was no other reason for him to be thinking such lustful thoughts about his king's daughter. Especially now that King Michael was missing and presumed dead.

Across the table Dominique was feeling a bit disturbed by Marcus's close scrutiny. It wasn't like him to look at her so intensely. And though she knew it was a crazy notion, she wondered if the man was finally seeing her as a woman. Not as the teenager he used to know.

The whole idea heated Dominique's cheeks and forced her to rise to her feet and put a measurable space between them.

Walking to the edge of the balcony, she leaned against the thick balustrade. From this high point, Old Stanbury, the capital city of Edenbourg, lay far below. Its network of winding narrow streets were nestled against green hillsides and lined with shops, boutiques and quaint cottages built centuries before the ravages of World War II had threatened this small island country.

Far to the west, between a break in the mountains, was a sparkling glimpse of blue-gray sea, while directly below were the palace grounds, where slopes of grassy lawns were dotted with huge shade trees and patterned with hedgerows. In another month, tea roses would be blooming thickly in the carefully tended gardens. A beautiful time for a wedding. But that part of Dominique's dreams were over.

She was trying to fight off those bitter thoughts when Marcus came to stand beside her. With a rueful smile, she looked over at him.

"I'm sorry, Marcus. I'm not very good company this morning."

The smile he cast her was regretful. "I'm not here to be entertained, Dominique. In fact, I think I should be the one apologizing for starting your day out on such a bad note.''

She drew in a deep breath, then let it out slowly. ''No. Please don't apologize. I want you to keep me abreast of what's happening with the investigation.''

He nodded soberly. ''Perhaps we'll hear something soon.''

As she studied his somber face, it suddenly dawned on her that her father's disappearance was bound to be tearing at him just as much as it was her. Marcus had spent many years serving his country and, most of all, his king. He had become her father's right-hand man, a close friend and confidant to Michael Stanbury.

The need to comfort him overshadowed her intentions to remain distant. She reached for his hand and gave it an encouraging squeeze. ''I know you must be hurting over all this, too, Marcus. You love Father very much.''

''Yes,'' he said flatly. ''It's not the same without him.''

''No. But then our lives never really stay the same, even when we want them to.''

Her comment brought a grimace to his face. ''I'm sure you heard about my marriage and divorce.''

She nodded while trying to hide her surprise that he'd brought up the subject. From what she recalled, Marcus had been a private man. She'd not expected him to want to share that sort of thing with anyone.

''It was in the papers,'' she told him. ''I couldn't help but see all the articles. I'm sorry things didn't work out for you.''

Pulling away from her, he gripped the top rail of the balustrade as he stared out at the distant city. ''Being a member of your father's staff made my private life fodder for the news media. I don't think there was even one story that ever got it right."

Her throat tightened with unexpected emotion. Marcus had always been a hero in her eyes. And heroes weren't ever supposed to hurt. "Your wife—I mean, ex-wife—is very beautiful. You must have loved her madly."

The corners of his mouth turned downward. Madly was probably the perfect way to describe his feelings toward Liza back then, Marcus thought. For a while he'd been insane over the woman. He'd not been able to see beyond his own besotted emotions that she was not suited to him or his way of life. Liza had never been able to understand that when duty to his country called, she had to take second stage.

"I'm over Liza, Dominique. But I do still deeply regret that our baby didn't survive."

*Baby.* The word jolted the deepest part of her and for long moments she was too choked to speak.

Finally, she managed, but her voice was hoarse and so low it was almost carried away with the sea breeze. "You'll have a child someday, Marcus. When you find that special woman."

His lips twisted to a mocking slant. "No. Two years ago Liza suffered a spontaneous miscarriage. The doctors couldn't explain why it happened. Except that nature had decided to intervene. Somehow the lack of a concrete reason made it harder for both of us to accept the loss. The whole thing made me realize that having a wife and a child of my own was...too risky an endeavor. I've decided I'm not cut out to be a husband or father. Some men aren't, you know."

Oh yes, Dominique did know. But she'd learned the

lesson too late. Now she had to face the reckoning of her folly alone.

Dominique was so lost in her problems, she wasn't aware that Marcus had moved closer until his lips were brushing a soft kiss against her cheek.

"Welcome home, Dominique," he murmured.

Too stunned to make any sort of reply, she watched him leave the balcony, then with quivering fingers, she touched the spot where his lips had warmed her skin.

Marcus believed he wasn't meant to be a husband or father. If Dominique was wise, she would make herself believe it, too.

Four days later, in the family room of the Stanbury palace, Dominique announced that she intended to drive out to the scene of her father's accident and have a look for herself.

"Dominique," Queen Josephine calmly spoke up, "the police are doing all they can. Your interference would only hinder their progress."

Dominique turned an astounded look on her perfectly groomed mother. Sometimes Josephine's stiff upper lip infuriated her. Putting on a strong and reserved facade for the public was one thing, but in the privacy of family, Dominique didn't believe any of them had to keep up a show of iron will.

Her parents had been married for thirty-three years and had produced three children together. Yet there had been times when Dominique wondered about their relationship. Their marriage had been an arrangement, made between two families seeking to merge their bloodlines and further enforce their power.

Now, as she looked at her mother sitting calmly in a winged-back chair, her smooth profile turned toward the flames in the fireplace, she could only guess at the woman's guarded emotions. Was she mourning a lost love or simply accepting that the king was dead and it was her duty to continue without him?

"What progress are you talking about, Mother? It's been a week and they still can't tell us what happened with Father! They can't even find his body!"

"That hardly means you can," Nicholas spoke up from across the room.

Dominique rolled her eyes toward the high ceiling of the massive room. "I didn't say I could, Nick. I'm only saying I want to go look for myself. I want to see where my father supposedly lost his life."

"Not me," Rebecca said from a nearby armchair. "It gives me the shivers just thinking about it."

"I'm with Rebecca. The scene is not something for the fainthearted to see."

This was from Jake Stanbury. Close to thirty years old with a tall, lean build and dark brown hair, he was the second son of Edward, who had arrived later that morning after the king's accident. In fact, he claimed he'd driven up on the scene shortly after it had happened and was credited with notifying the police.

Dominique didn't actually know either of her American cousins or her Uncle Edward. Nor was she yet sure what to make of their unannounced arrival in Old Stanbury. Especially on the very day of her father's accident. But Josephine had immediately welcomed them home and set them up in apartments on the palace grounds. With their mother setting that sort of cordial tone, Dominique had kept her doubts to herself and since then treated the three men as family. Nicholas and Isabel also appeared to be getting along with their American relatives.

"I'm not exactly fainthearted," Dominique said to Jake. "I can take a jolt."

Several feet away, Marcus rose from a high-back divan and joined Dominique in the middle of the room. Earlier he'd stopped by the family living quarters to discuss a foreign-trade agreement with Nicholas, but had wound up staying longer once the subject of the accident had been brought up.

For the past few minutes he'd been discreetly watching Dominique move restlessly around the room. Her outward appearance was elegant in a dove-gray skirt and a pale pink sleeveless sweater. A single strand of pearls rested against her neck and a pearl ring circled with diamonds adorned her right hand. But though she looked quite beautiful, he could sense a tightly controlled tenseness about her which worried him. Of all the Stanburys, she seemed to be taking the loss of King Michael the hardest, and that bothered him more than he cared to admit.

"Dominique, if you want to go out to the scene that badly, I'll take you myself. I have a few questions of my own about this investigation. Seeing the scene might help answer them," he offered.

Grateful for his support, she looked at him with relief. "I wouldn't want to put you out, Marcus. But if you'd really like to go, I'm certainly game."

He smiled at her, then glanced at his wristwatch. "Just let me go home and change my clothes. I'll pick you up in the courtyard in fifteen minutes."

Ten minutes later Dominique was ready and standing in wait on the stone driveway at the back of the castle. When Marcus pulled up beside her in a classic little MGB, she didn't wait for him to get out and open her door. She slid into the car and greeted him with a wide, grateful smile.

"You don't know what a reprieve you've given me." She spoke while buckling her seat belt. "I think I would have exploded if I hadn't gotten out of there soon."

Marcus put the sleek convertible into gear and headed them back across the drawbridge and on to the road to Old Stanbury.

"Nicholas tells me you haven't been out of the palace since your father's accident," he commented.

Her sigh was weary. "No. And the place is beginning to get to me." Grimacing, she glanced over at him. "I mean, not that I don't like my home. But, I suppose the university has been my home for so long now that, well, I'm just not use to the confinement here at the palace. Or being constantly observed by my family. Even Pru smothers me."

"The accident has put a strain on everyone, Dominique. I believe your mother is coping by trying to put the whole thing out of her mind."

Her frown deepened as she considered his words. "She's just so damn unfeeling at times I want to scream."

He smiled indulgently. "Your mother was bred to be strong. No matter what was thrown her way."

"Maybe so. But I happen to think the people of Edenbourg expect to see a queen weeping with tears of loss for her husband."

He turned his head slightly and looked at her with an arched eyebrow. "Because that's what you want to see from her?"

Dominique thought about his question for a moment. "I only know if I'd been married to a man for thirty-three years and borne him three children, I'd be stricken with grief.''

Yes, he could see where Dominique would be different from her mother, Marcus thought. Josephine was a rigidly controlled woman, whereas Dominique had appeared to grow into a passionate person. And something told him that if she did ever give her heart to a man, it would be totally, not just halfway.

"Perhaps Josephine just hides her emotions well. Some of us do.''

A glance at him suddenly reminded her of how close together the confines of the British car had put them. His shoulder was only a hand's span from hers, and even though the vinyl top was up and the day overcast, she was near enough to see the pores in his skin and the faint afternoon shadow of his dark beard. He'd changed into khakis and a pale yellow oxford shirt. The cuffs were rolled back against forearms lightly fuzzed with fine black hair. The collar and first button of the shirt were not fastened and to her own dismay she found herself trying to peep between the loosened folds of fabric.

"Does that mean when you were going through your divorce you kept your feelings hidden? Even from your family?'' she asked him.

The road had become steep and narrow. Marcus downshifted the car and kept his gaze firmly on the oncoming traffic.

"My family is just my father now. I have no brothers or sisters, if you recall. Mother died a couple years back. Complications from diabetes. At the time of my divorce, Father really wasn't in any shape to deal with all my problems. I kept most of them concealed from him. Thankfully, we're both doing better now.''

Was he? Dominique wondered. He'd just admitted to keeping his feelings to himself. Maybe he was still grieving for his wife and child. Maybe the pain was hidden from his eyes and camouflaged by his brief smiles. The idea bothered her greatly and she wondered just who or what it would take to get inside Marcus Kent.

Nearly thirty minutes passed before they reached the spot where the king's car had crashed through the heavy metal railing that guarded the narrow, twisting highway.

Because the police and other intelligence forces were still investigating the site, the road was blocked and the cliffside cordoned off with bright yellow tape. Marcus was forced to leave the MGB far back down the mountain road and the two of them walked the remaining distance until stopped by an officer in a dark blue uniform.

Marcus quickly presented him with his identification and then Dominique's. After studying it closely, the young officer went from abrupt and suspicious to embarrassed and fumbling all over himself.

"I didn't realize you were with the royal family," he said, then blushing, he swept off his hat and glanced sheepishly at Dominique. "I mean, I didn't recognize you, Princess Dominique. Nor you, Mr. Kent."

"I'm glad to see you're doing your job and making no exceptions," Marcus assured him. "Is it all right if we have a look around? We'll try not to disturb anything or get in the way."

"Of course," he said, then practically clicking his heels with attention, he lifted the tape to usher them under. "I'll let everyone else know who you are so that you won't be bothered."

The two of them thanked the officer then moved on.

As they walked, Marcus teased, "How does it feel to be an unrecognized princess?"

She smiled. "Actually, I like it. I've never wanted to be fawned over. As if I were more special than the next person. I'm not. I happened to be born to the king and queen. If not for that, I'd be just like any other woman in Edenbourg."

No, Marcus thought. She would never be like just any woman in this small country. Or anywhere else for that matter. She had a regal bearing, a beauty and compassion about her that made her stand out above others. The fact that she was so unpretentious made her even more appealing as a person.

Suddenly aware that she was no longer at his side, he paused and glanced back to see she'd stopped on the soggy cliffside. Her hands were planted on slender hips encased in dark blue jeans. A puzzled frown creased her forehead as she studied the highway running several yards up above them.

Stepping back to her, he asked, "What are you thinking?"

Watching her draw a deep breath, then let it out slowly, Marcus decided this whole place was cutting into her with vicious reality. Perhaps it had been a mistake to bring her out here, he thought ruefully. But for the past few days he'd watched her struggle to understand why she was now without her father. He wanted to help her come to grips with the accident and he'd hoped this little trip might help.

She looked at him thoughtfully. "It suddenly struck me that this particular road isn't the only route Father could have taken to the abbey the morning of the christening. In fact, the other road is shorter. And being inland, it's not nearly as treacherous as this."

He nodded in agreement. "I had already considered that, Dominique. And you're right. But for some reason King Michael must have chosen this route. Or he might have simply allowed the driver to choose which road he wanted to travel. I've seen him do that often in the past. Especially when he has business on his mind."

"You could be right," Dominique said as she glanced around her. "Mother does admit that he had some sort of last-minute business to attend to that morning. That's the reason he sent her on to the abbey without him. I just wonder what could have been so important."

Marcus's gazed drifted out to the choppy sea. "No one seems to know. There weren't any messages left on his phone. No scribbled notes on his desk. The night before, he didn't mention anything to me. I've tried to think of a pressing issue that might have come up suddenly, but I keep coming up with a blank."

Dominique sighed as she fought with strands of hair whipping into her face. It was a raw afternoon and she was glad she'd taken the time to change into jeans and a green, long-sleeved sweater. The tangy salt air had nipped her cheeks and nose and she knew without looking they had already turned as pink as her bare fingers.

Stuffing her hands into her jeans' pockets for warmth, she looked at Marcus and said, "Well, I can't help thinking the business might have had something to do with him traveling this road."

Shrugging a shoulder, he said, "You could be right, Dominique. But it would be impossible to make any sort of connection, unless we can figure out who or what King Michael had been attending to that morning."

"That's true," she agreed. "And don't you find it a bit more than strange that Jake Stanbury was traveling this same road? From what he's saying, he couldn't have been but a few minutes behind the accident."

"Yes. But with only his two-year-old son to corroborate his story, I'm not sure I want to put that much stock in it," Marcus admitted ruefully.

"Neither do I," Dominique agreed. "Edward and Luke's whereabouts seem fishy to me, too. Edward told Mother they had stopped off somewhere downtown before driving on to the abbey that morning. But I heard Luke say they were still at the airport when the accident occurred." She shook her head regretfully. "It's awful to be suspicious of your own relatives, Marcus. Especially when they've all continued to be so kind to us."

"I'm hoping Edward and his sons are truly here to make amends with the family. And so far I haven't detected anything to doubt their sincerity. But I'm not going to close my eyes completely where those three men are concerned."

The mere notion that her American relatives might have some connection to her father's accident sent a shiver of icy disbelief down Dominique's spine.

Sensing her distress, Marcus put a steadying hand against her back and urged her away from the edge of the cliffs. "Come along. Let's take a closer look and see what we can find before we start incriminating anyone."

# Chapter Three

The side of the cliff Dominique and Marcus were climbing was mostly grassy slopes broken up by rocky crevices and huge jagged boulders. At the point where the car had left the highway, it had traveled for several yards on smooth grass. The deep ruts from the tire tracks were still evident in the soggy turf.

The two of them noted the tracks were strangely straight, as though the driver hadn't tried to cut the wheel to the right or the left in an attempt to halt the car's destructive downward path.

At the end of the ruts, they reached a ledge of rock. Peering over the edge, they found a vertical drop of at least twenty feet to a bed of more jagged rocks. Black stains marred several of the boulders and from the plowed-up condition of the ground around them, Dominique knew this was where the car had made its final plunge before it crashed and burned.

The idea of her father and his driver perishing on the wild sea cliff was almost too much for Dominique. With a cry of anguish, she turned to Marcus and buried her face against his chest.

"Oh, Marcus, I can't believe my father died down there."

His arms came around her and pressed her against the warming comfort of his body. Her slender shoulders were trembling and her fingers clutched at his shirtfront. Never before had Marcus wanted to take away someone's pain so badly. Dominique was too soft, too precious to ever hurt this much.

Pressing his cheek against the top of her head, he whispered, "I shouldn't have brought you here. Seeing this place is only causing you more grief."

Dominique wanted to burst into sobs, but she bit them back and squeezed her eyes tightly shut. He believed she was distraught over her father. And she was. Yet she couldn't confide the whole truth of the matter to him. She couldn't tell him that losing her father was only a part of the worries weighing down on her shoulders.

Marcus was a gentleman. A man of honor and integrity. He was going to be shocked and disappointed that she'd not behaved in a manner of her breeding. His opinion of her, which had always meant so much, was going to nose-dive. Once he found out about her condition, he would probably shun her. And she wasn't quite ready for that. She needed his strength. More than he could ever know.

Shaking her head, she gulped down a sob. Then with another determined swallow, she leaned her head back far enough to allow her a view of his face. The wind had whipped his black hair across his forehead and ruddied his dark complexion. Compassion and regret clouded his golden-brown eyes, making her feel even more ashamed of herself.

"No," she said hoarsely. "Please don't feel badly about bringing me here. I'm glad you did."

He frowned. "Glad? You're trembling like a leaf, Dominique. You're upset."

"Yes. But I'm also a little relieved."

His expression somber, he studied her face for long moments. "Because now you can accept that your father is really dead?"

"No. Because now I'm more certain than ever that he didn't perish in this accident."

His hand lifted to tenderly stroke her windblown hair. "Dominique," he began doubtfully, "I know that you—"

Before he could finish, she twisted around in the circle of his arms and motioned toward the sight farther below them to where the ocean crashed upon the rock-strewn shoreline. Some distance out, several Coast Guard vessels bobbed on the cold, frothy waters of the North Sea.

"For the past seven days, special divers have been searching for a sign of King Michael's body or a part of the remains," she said. "So far they have found nothing. And I don't believe they will."

Marcus was trying to concentrate on her words, but it was a very hard thing to do when the warmth of her slender curves was radiating into his. Her hair carried the scent of wildflowers and tangy sea air and he found himself wanting to put his hands on her shoulders and draw her back against him. He wanted to dip his face into her hair, press his cheek against the regal line of her throat and draw in the womanly smell of her skin.

Dear Lord, he was losing all common sense, he

thought. He wasn't some sort of Romeo that chased after women years younger than himself. He didn't chase after women period. In fact, since Liza had divorced him, he'd vowed never to let his head be turned by another one.

Allowing himself to think such physical thoughts about Dominique scared him like nothing had in ages. It was indecent and improper and downright crazy on his part. He had to get a grip on himself and fast.

Gruffly, he cleared his throat, then purposely set her aside from him. Staring out at the rough seas, he forced himself to remember his dead king and the allegiance he owed him even now.

"What makes you think they won't find King Michael's body? Do you know something all these investigators don't?" he asked her.

She flushed at his question, but refused to relent. "I know it probably sounds absurd to you, Marcus. I'm just a naive young woman who doesn't know anything about accident scenes or investigations. But King Michael is my father. And I know I would feel something more if he were truly dead. Something inside would tell me to let him go and say goodbye. Besides," she added more firmly, "just take a look down there where the car finally landed. The whole area is surrounded by high boulders. It would be highly improbable that his body continued to roll down to the sea. The rocks would have prevented such a thing."

Trying to keep an open mind about all points of view was one of the reasons Marcus had risen to the lofty position of king's high counsel. Not that his quick intelligence hadn't helped. It had. But smartness wasn't the final thing that had propelled him into the prestigious job. It had been his ability to look at things from all angles that had singled him out and set him above the others serving on the king's administrative staff.

Now he reminded himself that Dominique's theories were not all that different than a political issue to be debated. It would serve him well to consider her opinion before closing his mind.

"All right," he said after a lengthy survey of the rock-strewn ledge below them. "I see what you mean. The boulders do more or less create a barrier of sorts. But that still doesn't explain what happened to King Michael's body. Unless it was totally cremated by the fire."

She came to stand a few inches from his side. He glanced over to see a frown puckering her features.

"The driver's body wasn't totally destroyed by the heat. There's no reason to think Father's was."

He grimaced at the horrid thought. "Except that he would have been sitting in the back. Closer to the petrol tank."

She shook her head, then with another idea glanced around for a spot on the ledge where they might climb over. "Do you think there's any chance we could climb down there for a closer look?"

He couldn't believe her tenacity and determination. But because he admired both qualities, he could hardly refuse her.

Who was he kidding? Marcus wondered. From the moment he'd spotted her in the abbey the morning of the christening, he'd been struck silly by the sight of her. Each time he looked at her, he wanted to lay the world at her feet. He wanted to see happiness radiating from her face and know that he'd been the sole reason for putting it there.

"It looks like a difficult climb. Are you sure you want to go down there?" he asked.

"I'm game for it. And we might see something the police overlooked," she added on a hopeful note.

Nicholas and the queen would certainly frown if they heard about this, Marcus thought. But he hadn't come out to this place for their benefit. He was here for Dominique's peace of mind. And whether that was a good or bad reason, he hadn't yet decided.

With a groan of acquiescence, he held up his hands. "I'm glad your sister, Isabel, isn't here with us. Otherwise she'd be ready to scramble down the side of this cliff with you."

"Darn right," Dominique said with a grin. "She's no softy. And neither am I."

"Okay, Miss Adventuress, let's see if we can find a trail to follow where we're least likely to break our necks."

More than thirty minutes later they finally reached the actual crash sight. Other than a few scraps of torn metal and exposed earth there was nothing more to see. It was the thing they weren't seeing that struck Marcus the most.

Below the curvature of boulders, the path down to the sea was for the most part grassy and more gently sloping than the upper two-thirds of the cliff. If King Michael's body had been flung from the car and somehow gotten over the boulders, the grass and rain-sodden earth past them would have been disturbed by the fall. Yet there were no signs or marks indicating something or someone had tumbled over the area.

"See what I mean, Marcus?"

The simple question brought him out of his deep

thoughts. He glanced at her, his expression grim and thoughtful. "Yes, I see what you mean."

"What do you think now?"

Closing his eyes for a moment, he pinched the bridge of his nose. "I'm not sure what to think." Dropping his hand from his face, he gazed out at the Coast Guard ships. They were using sonar and other sophisticated underwater radar devices, along with the human eye, to search the ocean floor lying along the site of the accident and beyond. Whether those guards believed they had good reason for their search, Marcus couldn't say. But so far they'd turned up little more than the rusty frames of a few old sunken fishing boats.

"If Michael wasn't killed in the accident, then there's something very sinister going on."

She shivered. And not from the gusty wind or the smattering of raindrops that had begun to sting her face.

"Are you going to say anything to my family about this?"

He looked over to see her wrapping both arms around her waist in an effort to warm herself. Before he let himself think about what he was doing, he reached out and curled his arm around her shoulders.

"No. If there is something else going on here besides a simple car accident, it will surface. Right now they would think we both needed to be scheduled for mental therapy. And in my position, it wouldn't look good if I'd appeared to have lost my wits."

He ended his words with a rueful smile and suddenly Dominique laughed and reached for his hand.

Giving it a squeeze, she said, "Oh, Marcus, the sight of this place struck me hard a few minutes ago. But now I can't help feeling a ray of hope. Thank you for bringing me here."

She suddenly rose on tiptoe and kissed his cheek. The intimate gesture caught Marcus by total surprise and he stared down at her with a mixture of affection and bewilderment.

"I don't know that I deserved that kiss or your thanks. It's starting to rain and we've got a long climb back to the car."

Laughing, she glanced up at the slate-gray sky as fat raindrops began to smatter them from all directions.

"I think you're right," she said. "We'd better hurry."

She tugged on his hand to urge him to follow after her. Marcus held on to her fingers and wondered why it felt as though she'd also just tugged on his heart.

Even by quickening their pace, it took the two of them close to an hour to climb back up the slippery cliff, then down the highway to where they'd left the car. Thankfully, by then the rain had slackened. Otherwise, the two of them would have been drenched to the skin. Instead, their clothes were only damp.

"There's a jacket behind the passenger seat. Put it on," he told her as he started the car. "It'll make you a bit warmer."

As he put the little convertible in motion, Dominique rummaged behind her and pulled out a black poplin jacket lined with warm fuzzy flannel. Quickly, she plunged her arms into the sleeves and sighed as the warmth of the garment surrounded her.

"I wasn't expecting the weather to turn so nasty. I should have had more forethought and brought a jacket with me," she told him as she snuggled down into the bucket seat.

"I'll get the heater going in a moment. And we're

only thirty minutes away from the castle." He cast her a brief, pondering glance. "Or would you like to stop off downtown and have something warm to drink first?"

Dominique's face was suddenly lit with undisguised pleasure. "Oh, could we? A change of scene from the castle would be lovely. Do you have time?"

Even though there wasn't anything on his desk that needed urgent attention, her question caused him a pang of guilt. It was Liza he was thinking of now and how she'd continually accused him of not taking enough time out of his busy work schedule to spend with her.

To a certain point, she'd been right. Marcus had always put his job first. After all, he'd given his allegiance to serve the king long before he'd married Liza. But she'd expected him to give her the same sort of loyalty and devotion. He'd tried. But a man could just spread himself so thin before something started to break. In the end it had been his marriage.

So if he'd not had time for Liza, what was he doing spending this afternoon with Dominique? he asked himself. Inviting more trouble for himself? She was off-limits to him. He shouldn't be flirting with her. Even in a harmless way.

"Marcus, you're frowning. What is it? Have you decided you need to get back to the castle, after all?"

With a shake of his head, he glanced at Dominique. Her face was fresh and sweet and so unlike the wife who'd divorced him. Liza had been all glamour, with ink-black hair, deep blue eyes and lips that were always painted a vivid red or bright coral. She'd been a beautiful siren. And when they'd first met, he'd not been able to resist her. That had been his biggest mistake.

One that he was still paying for. Not with his wallet but with emotional scars that refused to fade.

The memories filled him with disgust and twisted his lips to a rueful line. "No. I don't have to go back to the castle right now. I was just thinking about my ex-wife," he admitted. "She believed I neglected her."

Dominique's eyebrows lifted ever so slightly as she searched his dark profile. Once again, she'd not expected him to unload something so personal. But then the stress of the past week was causing everyone to behave out of character. She wasn't foolish enough to believe she had anything to do with Marcus opening his private life.

After a moment, she decided to ask, "Did you?"

His jaw tightened. "Not intentionally. I never wanted to hurt her that way. But my job kept me confined to the castle and she hated that. Especially after she became pregnant."

Dominique was almost glad she'd been away while Marcus had been married. Somehow she knew it would have hurt to see him with another woman or to see that woman carrying his child. She'd even gone so far as to dream that once she grew up and acquired her education, she would come back and wow him with her beauty and poise and dignity.

Dignity, she silently repeated with a healthy dose of self-disgust. That trait was the last thing she possessed. And soon the whole world was going to know it.

Trying to take her thoughts elsewhere, she glanced at him and asked, "Was my father that much of a slave driver? I know he can be very demanding. Nicholas and Isabel have certainly had their own rounds with him. And I've had a few in the past. But being away at university has spared me many of his edicts."

His sigh was followed by a smile of genuine fondness. "No. King Michael never asked more of me than he would have asked of himself. If I needed time away from the office, he didn't question my reasons."

She continued to search his profile while wondering just how much his heart had been broken. And she was sure it had been broken. Marcus might appear hard and cool to most people, but Dominique knew there was more to him once you got past the armored layer of skin.

"Then what was the problem?"

Funny, but if anyone else had asked him such a forward question he would have shot them down with a cool stare. But Dominique was different somehow. She made it feel normal for him to talk about his failings. And God knew, he'd had plenty where Liza was concerned.

"In simple terms, Dominique, I didn't know how to be a husband."

She thought about that as the car carried them into the busier streets of downtown. Finally, when he stopped at the first traffic light, she looked at him and asked, "Are you telling me you didn't know how to be a husband, or just didn't want to be?"

He answered with a good-natured chuckle. "Oh, Dominique, you are an inquisitive little thing."

Glad to see her questions hadn't offended him, she smiled. "That's how a person learns, you know. By asking questions."

He smiled back at her. "Hmm. I'll remember that in a few minutes. After I loosen your tongue with something warm to drink."

Even though Marcus was teasing, the comment was enough to make Dominique uneasy. If he asked her about her life at the university, she wasn't sure what she was going to say.

Don't be crazy, she silently scolded herself. There was plenty she could say about her studies and the friends she'd made there without bringing Bryce's name into things. And anyway, she seriously doubted Marcus would be interested in hearing about her love life. Not that there'd been much love involved where Bryce had been concerned, she thought grimly. Dominique was ashamed to admit it, but the feelings that had gone on between the two of them had all been misguided and very one-sided on her part.

But she didn't want to think about Bryce or any of that heartache now. Marcus was going out of his way to give her a few minutes of relaxation. She was going to do her best to enjoy it and try not to worry about what the near future was going to bring to her.

Moments later, Marcus parked on a steep and narrow cobblestone street, far away from the hustle and bustle of downtown shoppers and traffic.

Dominique gazed curiously through the windshield at the small inn. It was nothing like the modern fast-food places that had sprung up in the newer additions of the growing city in the past few years. This place was an authentic European cottage constructed of white stucco and a thatched roof. Green wooden shutters framed the paned windows. Directly below, in wooden boxes of the same color, yellow and purple pansies shouted to be noticed among tall red tulips. Above the heavy door which served as the entrance, hung an iron sign which read Chauncey's.

"I don't ever remember seeing this place," she told him. "But I should have. It's lovely."

"And quiet. That's the best part," he told her.

His remark brought another thought to her mind. She glanced anxiously over at him as he proceeded to unbuckle his seat belt.

"Marcus, do you think we should be doing this?"

He paused to look at her, his face wrinkled with confusion. "What do you mean, doing this?"

Suddenly feeling awkward, she shrugged. "Well, I wasn't thinking. Maybe I shouldn't be out and about in public like this right now. The news is already saturated with Father's disappearance. If they see the two of us, they'll probably report we were out kicking up our heels instead of properly mourning the king."

Scowling, he motioned for her to get out of her seat belt. "Don't worry about the news media, Dominique. It's very doubtful any sort of reporter will see us here. And even if they do, we're not going to worry about what they say. Even if King Michael is dead, we have to keep on living, don't we? We can't stop the world from going on around us while we wait for some sort of word."

She bit down on her bottom lip as she considered all he'd just said. "You're right, of course," she finally answered. "We can't remain hidden away in the castle forever. But people sometimes misconstrue what they see."

With his left arm propped on the steering wheel, he turned in the seat and leaned slightly toward her. Dominique instinctively swallowed as his very male presence enveloped her, filling her head with all sorts of erotic fantasies.

"What are they going to see, Dominique? The king's daughter and his high counsel having a drink on a cold afternoon? I don't see what could be misconstrued about that."

Her gaze fell to her lap, where her fingers were gripping the edges of his jacket. It wasn't fair that he made her feel so edgy, so aware of being a woman. Especially when she appeared to have no such effect on him at all.

The whole idea filled her with frustration, and before she could stop herself, she was saying, "No. You wouldn't see where anyone might put the two of us together. Because you don't see me—as a woman." She lifted her head and darted him a look that dared him to deny her words. "But I am, Marcus. And you're a divorced man."

He rolled his eyes, scoffing at the idea that anyone would dare link them in such a way. His attitude hurt. Probably more than if he'd whacked her with his hand. She might not possess the beauty of his ex-wife, but she wasn't unappealing to look at. She'd turned several male heads at the university. They just hadn't belonged to someone as mature or forceful as Marcus.

Disbelief twisted his features. "Don't be ridiculous! You're years younger than me. And a princess of Edenbourg at that. I'm a commoner. You'd never settle for anything less than a duke or marquess for a husband."

She looked at him with raised eyebrows. "Why think they would link us together in that manner? They might just say we're having an affair."

He looked absolutely angry now.

"Oh, good Lord, Dominique!"

Quickly, she heaved out a breath and jerked off her seat belt. "You're right. How silly of me to imagine someone like you would look at someone like me for a lover! I'm not nearly glamorous enough to be a mistress. My qualifications are only good for the dowdy wife of a boring blue blood!"

Before Marcus had time to get out of the car and come around to her door, she'd opened it herself and climbed out on the wet cobblestone.

He slid out of the car and went around to where she stood, but she purposely refused to look at him. Taking a firm grip on her elbow, he said, "You're being childish now, Dominique. And what, pray tell me, brought on such an outburst from you?"

Humiliation burned her cheeks. Tears scalded her throat. What in heaven's name had come over her? she wondered wildly. How could she have linked their names with the word *lover?* Now he was going to think she was still nursing a childish crush on him. After four long years!

With a soft groan of anguish, she closed her eyes and shook her head. "I'm sorry, Marcus. I don't know what made me say those things. Please forget it. Please."

For long moments he studied her bowed head, then he heaved a heavy breath and nudged her toward the inn. "Come on," he said gruffly. "It's starting to rain again."

# *Chapter Four*

Inside the rustic tavern only a handful of patrons sat at tiny square wooden tables covered with blue-checked cloths. Farm-type lanterns hung from the low-beamed ceiling and fat nubby candles flickered from the center of each table, providing meager light in the dark interior. The scent of fish and chips and ale lingered in the warm air, and as Marcus guided her through the maze of tables, Dominique's stomach reacted by quickly rising in her throat.

Panicked with the realization that she was going to be sick, she stopped in her tracks and jerked her elbow free from his grip.

Marcus glanced down at her with further annoyance. "What's—"

"I'm sorry, Marcus, but I—I have to find the ladies' room."

Before he could ask more, she whirled and hurried away toward a rest-room sign hanging behind the bar in a far corner of the inn.

After nearly running through the maze of tables, Dominique locked herself inside the small facilities, then lost every bit of the lunch she'd eaten before leaving the castle.

As she heaved over the commode, she tried not to think of Marcus waiting on her or how she was going to look once she did go back out to join him. Her head was swimming with nausea, and sweat drenched her face and neck.

Several minutes passed before she was able to sponge her face with a damp paper towel and bring some semblance of order to her disheveled hair.

Above the tiny sink, a foggy mirror reflected a young woman with a paper-white face, hollow eyes and pinched mouth. But Dominique accepted the fact that there was nothing she could do about her appearance now. She'd not bothered to bring a purse with her on this outing, much less a compact of pressed powder or a tube of lipstick.

Besides, how she looked to Marcus wasn't nearly as bad as what she'd said to him. But it was too late to take back the words. Too late to take back a lot of things, she thought grimly.

With that in mind, Dominique squared her shoulders and left the sanctity of the rest room. She immediately saw Marcus sitting at one of the tables in the opposite corner of the dimly lit room. A redheaded waitress stood over him, a pad in one hand and a pencil in the other. But from the animated expression on her face, Dominique could see the woman wasn't in a hurry to take his order.

Easing into the wooden chair directly across from him, Dominique felt both Marcus and the waitress eyeing her as if she had smut on her nose.

Pretending indifference, she asked, "Have you ordered for me?"

The faint lift of his eyebrows told her he'd been more worried about her running out a back exit of the building than trying to decide what she wanted to drink.

"No," he answered. "I decided you'd better choose your own poison."

Dominique took a deep breath and hoped the tabletop prevented him from seeing her hand pressed against her quivering stomach. "A ginger ale, please," she told the waitress.

Her choice put a confused frown on his face. "I thought you wanted something warm."

"I—I did, but it doesn't sound good now." She glanced at the waitress to make sure the woman wasn't confused about the order. "Keep it a ginger ale," she told her.

With a confirming nod, the redhead swished away. Across the table, Marcus's unsettling gaze continued to survey her as if he was seeing a person he didn't quite know. Dominique swallowed and stared out the paned window to the right of her. Rain was falling steadily now, darkening the street and the stone steps leading up to the entrance of the inn.

"You were gone so long I was getting ready to ask the waitress to check on you," he said.

She pushed a hand through her tumbled hair. "I'm sorry. I was feeling a bit sick and I waited for it to pass."

"You look like you've stuck your face in a bin of flour. Are you feeling all right now?" he asked.

There was no annoyance in his voice, only concern. For some reason she couldn't fathom, Marcus's caring attitude was harder to deal with than his anger.

Suddenly her eyes blurred with tears and she stared at the tabletop as she desperately tried to pull herself together.

"I'll be fine," she murmured in a wobbly voice. "It's—I've just been having a trying time here lately, Marcus. I guess the stress is getting to me."

She couldn't explain that her body was being bombarded with a heavy dose of unfamiliar hormones and that her moods sometimes swung from high to low in a matter of seconds. The least little thing brought tears to her eyes and words that she would never normally say sometimes spouted from her lips as if a stranger had taken over her body.

Her hand slid downward to the lower part of her belly and cupped the slight mound that had just become evident in the past few weeks. Another life had taken over her body, she realized. And though a part of her wanted to shout with joy that she was three months pregnant, she'd never been so terrified or torn in her life.

"If you're ill, we can forget the drinks and go back to the castle."

She sniffed, then wiping her cheeks with both hands, she lifted her head and forced herself to look at him. "No, I'm fine. Really, Marcus."

His expression skeptical, he leaned back in the wooden chair and crossed his arms over his chest. "I thought I knew you, Dominique. But I can see that I don't."

Her chin lifted to a faintly defensive angle. "We haven't really seen each other in over four years. I've changed. I've grown up since then."

His lips twisted to a mocking slant. "It didn't sound like it a few minutes ago."

Her nostrils flared and color splashed across her

cheeks as a spurt of anger renewed her strength. "I told you to forget that. What I was trying to say didn't come out right, that's all."

Dropping his arms, he leaned forward as if he was preparing to give her some sort of strong retort, but the sudden appearance of the waitress diverted his attention.

While Marcus was served a cappuccino and Dominique her ginger ale, she braced herself. She wasn't about to let Marcus think she still idolized him. She hadn't lost all pride!

"Dominique, I am a divorced man now. But that doesn't make me eligible to any woman. Especially you."

Thank goodness her tearful mood was over and anger was stiffening her spine. She wasn't going to let this man crush her feelings. Bryce had already done enough of that.

Her green eyes raked across the handsome angles and planes of his face. "I didn't realize you'd turned into a conceited man, Marcus. Do you think every woman in your company wants you in her bed?"

Disgust turned the corners of his mouth downward. "I wouldn't know. That's hardly a question I go around asking."

"Then why pick on me?"

His eyes widened and she knew their conversation wasn't turning in the direction he'd expected. Good, she thought. Marcus didn't need to think he could control everyone and especially her.

"Dominique!" he spurted with disbelief. "A while ago in the car you said—"

"I know what I said." She snapped the interruption. "That the news media might try to link us in a—carnal way. I was only trying to express my worries to you. But all you could do was insult me!"

With a tight grimace on his face, he reached for the mug of steaming cappuccino. "If I did, it's because you shouldn't even be thinking such things. Let alone saying them out loud. To me. You're still a child," he muttered.

No, Dominique thought. Her young innocent years were gone. She wasn't a child. She was *carrying* a child. And she was beginning to wonder if now might be the time to let Marcus Kent know exactly how grown-up she had become and what a scandalous mess she'd gotten herself into.

"Tell me, Marcus, what determines a person's leap from childhood to adulthood? Chronological age? If so, I'm twenty-one. I've reached that legal mark on the calendar."

"The number has nothing to do with it," he said, his voice gruff with frustration.

Her lips twisted mockingly. "When you were my age, I'm sure you considered yourself a man."

"Of course I did. But I didn't know enough about life to really be a man. That takes time and the wisdom that comes with it."

Slowly her gaze scanned his dark features. He believed she was still an innocent young woman who knew very little about the harsh realities of the world. She could only imagine how shocked he was going to be once she spilled her secret.

But would learning she was carrying a child be enough to convince Marcus she had grown both mentally and physically into womanhood? she wondered. Somehow she doubted it. She'd always known him to be a sober man who never did anything on impulse or yielded to frivolity. His decisions were always carefully weighed. He would never allow passion to rule his head. And because she had, he would probably consider her even more immature and foolish than he did at this very moment.

"How much does a person have to know, Marcus?" she asked softly. "How much pain or sorrow or joy must I feel before I can truly say I'm a woman?"

Irritation at her persistence caused his features to tighten. He glanced at her, then at the falling rain beyond the window. "I don't know, Dominique."

"Then how do you know I'm still a child?" she insisted.

His gaze swung back to her face, and though the thrust of his jaw remained unrelenting, she could see in his eyes that he was trying to understand her.

"Why are you harping on this?"

A flush of pale pink swept across her high cheekbones. "I don't appreciate being belittled. Especially when you don't know—"

She broke off abruptly, horrified that she'd been about to blurt out that she was pregnant. What was she thinking? she wondered wildly. She couldn't tell Marcus now. He had enough worries trying to deal with the uproar of her father being missing and presumed dead. Not to mention trying to ease Nicholas into the responsibilities of the throne of Edenbourg.

"Don't know what?" he prodded.

Clamping her lips tightly together, she shook her head and looked away from him. "Forget it, Marcus. It wasn't important."

She could feel his gaze searching her profile, probing for answers she wasn't giving him.

"You were about to say something, Dominique. It

must have been important. Is there something you're not telling me? Something I should know?''

"No!" she said sharply, then reached for her glass. With a negligent shrug, she tried to feign a casualness she was far from feeling. "I was only going to say that you really don't know me."

His response was nothing more than a faint lift of his black eyebrows.

The reaction compelled her to go on, "I mean, I've been gone for a long time, Marcus. And a lot of things have happened to make me a different person than the young girl you used to know."

Suddenly a wry smile touched the corners of his mouth. "Since you've been away a lot has happened to me, too. Not all of it good."

He was talking about his divorce and she found herself wanting to tell him she'd learned all about loving a person, then losing him. About having her beliefs shattered by a man she'd trusted.

Yet she bit back the words partly out of dread and shame and partly because he wouldn't understand completely. Unless he knew about the baby.

She hoped he couldn't detect the trembling of her hand as she lifted the glass to her lips. After a few careful sips, she lowered the drink back to the table, then cast him a wan smile.

"Not everything has been good for me either, Marcus. Especially this past week."

The sudden reminder of Michael Stanbury's accident caused his expression to turn grave. "No. This past week hasn't been good for you or your family," he agreed.

Her gaze fell to the tabletop as sadness welled up inside of her. "Nor you, Marcus. Or anyone who loves Father." She looked up at him, her eyes full of shad-

ows. "I used to think everyone loved King Michael.
But now—" She shuddered as the memory of the accident scene rose up in her mind. "It seems incredible,
but I'm afraid I might have to accept the idea that someone out there meant him harm."

Grim-faced, Marcus swallowed the last of the cappuccino, then placed the mug on the table.

"If you're ready to go, I think we'd better head back
to the castle," he told her. "Your family will be worried
about you. And that's the last thing they need."

Yes, she thought miserably as she pushed aside the
half-empty glass of ginger ale. Worrying her family was
not something she wanted to do. But soon her belly was
going to resemble a large, ripe pumpkin. She wouldn't
be able to hide her condition from them or Marcus. Her
scandalous behavior would be gossiped about through
the whole countryside and her family would be helpless
to stop it.

"You're right," she agreed. "We should be getting
back or everyone will be thinking we've had an accident
in this weather."

And she needed to get away from him, Dominique
thought. Before she did something stupid and sobbed
everything out to him.

He came around the table and helped her from her
chair. As they left the little inn, Dominique was more
aware than ever of his warm hand on the back of her
arm, his tall, lean body only inches from her side.

As the two of them traveled the few miles back to
the castle, she tried not to think about the way she'd
felt out on the sea-swept cliff when he'd held her in his
arms. Those moments had been precious and it would
be dangerous for her to allow her thoughts to linger over
them.

"You're very quiet, Dominique. Are you angry with me?"

His voice pulled her out of her thoughts and she looked around to see they were quickly approaching the drawbridge leading into the castle grounds. Their trip home had been made in silence.

Something twisted inside her, sending a little pain between her breasts. "No. Of course I'm not angry."

She didn't look at him even when she heard him release a heavy sigh.

Once he braked the car to a halt, he reached over and gently touched her forearm. Beneath his fingers, her flesh sizzled and burned.

"I didn't mean to…belittle you, as you called it, Dominique. I guess it's hard for me to accept that not only is King Michael gone, but also his young daughter who used to smile shyly at me as we passed in the hallways."

His words affected her far more than they should have and her eyes were wet when she lifted them to his face. "Sometimes I miss that young girl, too, Marcus. Sometimes I wish I could go back to that time. But I can't. Nor can you."

Quickly, she unlatched her seat belt and let herself out of the car before he had the chance to see her foolish tears.

A few minutes later, Dominique entered her suite and found Prudence in the little study both women used as an office.

"Dominique, you're back! What did you—" The rest of Prudence's sentence was never uttered as she took one look at her princess's pale, pinched features. "What's wrong?"

Dominique sank wearily onto one end of a plush divan while Prudence hurried from behind a small desk. "Nothing is wrong, Pru," she said, trying her best not to sound cross, but knowing she did anyway.

The other woman stood with her hands on her hips, quietly surveying Dominique's appearance. "You look, well, frankly, you look horrible."

With both hands, Dominique pushed her tangled hair back from her face. "It was windy and raining out on the cliffs. I didn't think to take a jacket, and my hair and clothes got wet."

"You have a jacket on," Prudence pointed out.

Dominique glanced down at herself then silently groaned. She'd forgotten all about Marcus's jacket.

"Marcus lent it to me. I'll have to get it cleaned and sent back to him."

Not waiting for an invitation, Prudence sank down beside her on the divan. "Actually, I wasn't referring to your hair or clothes when I said you looked horrible. It's your face."

Dominique rolled her eyes. "Oh, well, you're really making me feel wonderful, Pru. Every woman wants to hear her face is a mess."

Prudence laughed softly. "I didn't mean—you're beautiful, Dominique. You only have to look in the mirror to see that." With a shake of her head, she peered more closely at Dominique. "Are you all right? You're so pale."

Dominique passed a weary hand over her face. She was so tired of pretending, so weary of hiding her feelings and worries. With every day that passed she was growing more and more exhausted. Sometimes she feared all the stress would harm the baby. Yet she didn't know how to alleviate any of it.

"I'm just tired, Pru. I'm fine, really. Don't fret about me."

Somewhat convinced, Prudence lost her worried look. Quickly, she scooted to the edge of the cushion and squared her knees around so that she was facing Dominique. "So tell me what happened," she urged with an eager smile.

Dominique frowned at the other woman. "For heaven's sake, Pru, you make it sound like I've been on a date!"

Prudence groaned with frustration. "Dominique, you haven't been away from the palace for probably two weeks. I only wanted to know how your afternoon went." She looked offended. "But if you don't want to tell me…"

If she kept mum it would only raise Prudence's suspicion that something had gone on between her and Marcus, and that was the last thing she wanted the other woman to think. Because nothing had. And he'd made it painfully obvious that nothing ever would.

Dominique reached over and gave Prudence's hand a quick, affectionate squeeze. "I'm sorry, Pru. I'm really sounding waspish and I don't mean to. I—seeing the scene of Father's accident was much harder than I imagined it would be. The cliff where the car went over is very steep and strewn with huge boulders. And the spot where the car actually burned—" A shudder rippled through her and she momentarily closed her eyes. "Even though the charred metal had already been taken away, I kept picturing it in my mind, wondering if my father really perished there."

Prudence's brown eyes widened at the suggestion of Dominique's words. "Don't you believe King Michael died in the accident? I realize they haven't found his body, but from what I've heard, the police believe it would have been impossible for anyone to have survived such a fall.''

That was true enough, Dominique thought. If King Michael had been in the car when it plunged over the cliff, he was most likely dead. But she wasn't quite convinced that her father had been in the vehicle. Still, she wasn't going to voice her doubts to Prudence. At least, not until the police released their whole findings on the matter.

''It does look impossible,'' Dominique agreed.

''Do you think the divers will find his body?''

Sighing, she leaned her head against the back of the divan. ''I have my doubts. So does Marcus.''

The mention of the man's name brought a sly smile back to Prudence's pretty face. ''So tell me about him,'' she urged.

Careful to keep her expression smooth, Dominique said, ''There isn't anything to tell. You know Marcus as well as I.''

''Oh, come on, Dominique! Neither one of us has forgotten what a major crush you had on the man before you left for college.''

Dominique shot her a vexed look. ''I was a teenager then. You had some silly crushes of your own during that time, too. Like the polo player from Roxbury who wore his spurs to tea.''

''True,'' Prudence agreed with a giggle. ''But mine was just that silly. Yours was, well, far too serious. In fact,'' she added shrewdly, ''I would be willing to bet that Marcus hasn't forgotten it either. You're a beautiful woman now. And he's a divorced man.''

Dominique groaned as she felt color flood her face. When she'd brought up the idea that people might link them romantically, he'd looked absolutely horrified. No, she thought resolutely, Marcus had made his feelings toward her clear. He wasn't eligible to any woman. Especially her.

"It's no wonder my parents separated you and me for such a long time," Dominique muttered. "You were always trying to put ridiculous ideas in my head. You still are."

Prudence's soft laugh was suggestive. "There's nothing ridiculous about Marcus Kent that I can see. He's quite a man in my book."

He was quite a man, Dominique silently agreed. That's why he'd been impossible to forget. Even now that she was carrying another man's child.

Disgusted with herself, she rose to her feet and started to the bedroom. She needed to get out of her damp clothes and get her mind off the king's high counsel.

"Maybe so," Dominique called over her shoulder. "But he's off-limits to me. And he always will be. Besides, I'm not interested in finding a man. Especially one as stubborn and controlling as Marcus Kent!"

At the same time, across the palace grounds, Marcus moved restlessly around his apartment. He was angry at himself. More angry than he could ever remember being. He didn't know what had come over him this afternoon. He'd wanted to hold Dominique in his arms and assure her that everything was going to be all right. But touching her silky hair, feeling her soft womanly body against his had turned his thoughts elsewhere and made him wonder what it would be like to make love to her.

It had been wrong of him to come down so hard on her when they'd stopped outside the inn and she'd talked about reporters linking them romantically. But her suggestion had only further echoed what he'd been feeling. And he'd not wanted to admit, even to himself, that there could ever be such a connection between them.

Cursing silently, he snatched up the morning paper and sat down in an armchair facing the small fireplace in the cozy den. Nicholas had urged him to take the rest of the afternoon off and he needed to make the most of it. Not pace around the apartment brooding about Dominique.

Snapping open the paper, he tried to focus on world and Edenbourg news, but the headlines were little more than a jumble of black letters. He couldn't concentrate on political happenings, the weather or sports, or anything else. Not with Dominique's sad, beautiful features swimming before his eyes.

With another silent oath, he tossed down the paper and walked over to a window that looked up at the east side of the castle where Dominique's rooms were located.

It wasn't like him to be so affected by a woman. In fact, since Liza had divorced him, he'd truly believed his interest in females had died. He'd not felt the need to have an intimate relationship with any woman. And so far he'd not even attempted to look for a casual companion, much less search for a lifetime soul mate.

He'd already learned he couldn't be a husband. Three-quarters of his time was spent at the king's side. The rest wasn't enough to hold any type of relationship together, much less a marriage. It would be crazy to even think of Dominique in the role of his wife. She was years younger than him. She was a princess, born and bred to marry an aristocrat. Not a commoner who'd come up the hard way. The two of them were worlds apart in class and age.

He thrust a hand roughly through his black hair as his gaze lifted to the turret that made up Dominique's bedroom. His desire for her this afternoon had been a shock and for a moment he'd forgotten himself. But he wouldn't allow his feelings to take control of him a second time. No, he was too old and wise to fall in love again. Especially with a beautiful princess.

# Chapter Five

Nearly a week later, Marcus sat in King Michael's office—a lofty room in the castle that looked down on the river that flowed through Old Stanbury and on to the sea. One whole wall of the elongated room was covered with photos of family and friends. The other three were lined with books, many of which had been handed down through the centuries from one Stanbury generation to the next. Marcus had always liked the room because it represented not only family love and loyalty, but also devotion to one's country. And even more, he was fond of the room because this was the place he had spent more time than any with Michael Stanbury, his king.

But today, Michael wasn't sitting behind the wide mahogany desk with a cup of tea in one hand and a phone in the other. It was his son who was diligently trying to fill the throne of Edenbourg.

"I hate to be the one to give you this news, your Highness," Marcus said to him, "but I've just received word that the divers have been sent home. Their commander tells me any more searching would be fruitless. And, frankly, I'm inclined to agree with him. They've been searching the waters for more than two weeks now and have so far come up with nothing.''

Across the wide desk, Nicholas looked regretfully at his friend and high counsel.

"Actually, I'm surprised they haven't thrown in the towel before now,'' he told Marcus. ''Especially with the squally weather we've been having.''

Marcus could see a fatal sort of acceptance settle over Nicholas's face. It was the same look he'd noticed on most everyone he'd encountered in the castle this past week. Except for Dominique. He'd made a point of not seeing her for any reason.

"I'm sure out of respect for your father none of the rescue team wanted to give up. But in the end common sense has to prevail.''

Nicholas let out a long breath of resignation. "Well, I guess that means the book is closed on the accident now.''

Marcus absently drummed his fingers against his knee. Even though days had passed since he and Dominique had driven out to the cliffs, he'd not shared their suspicions about the accident with anyone. And he was safely sure that she'd not voiced them to anyone either. The knowledge left him feeling oddly connected to her, even though he'd not spoken with her since that day.

"Not necessarily,'' Marcus carefully replied. ''There's still hope the autopsy on the driver will uncover some sort of new lead.''

Nicholas tossed down the pen he was holding. "Hell, Marcus, the man burned to death. What more is there for the coroner to say?''

"It's impossible to predict. Forensic science has taken great strides in the past few years. Who knows, tests might show the driver was drunk."

Nicholas snorted mockingly. "Herbert drunk? The man was as solid as a rock. The strongest thing he ever drank was tea doused with goat cream."

Marcus smiled with fond remembrance of the driver who'd been a permanent fixture for as long as he could remember here at Stanbury castle. He'd been a wiry little man in his sixties and had liked to relate tales of his early days in the Royal Navy.

"How do you know Herbert put goat cream in his tea?"

Thoughtful now, Nicholas rubbed a thumb against his chin. "Because I've heard Gertie, the cook in the kitchen, scolding him for getting into the cream she used to make cheese."

"Maybe Gertie wanted to teach him a lesson and put something in the cream to make him sick."

Marcus had merely been joking but Nicholas seemed to take him seriously. But then everybody had always taken him in a grave sort of way. As though the idea of him making light of anything was impossible. He suddenly wondered if Dominique viewed him in the same manner. Stiff, wooden and incapable of laughing at life.

"Oh no, Marcus. Gertie loved Father. And as far as that goes, Herbert, too. She's been sick with grief."

Marcus swiftly shook his head. "I didn't mean it seriously, Your Majesty. In fact, I know Gertie loved King Michael. Most everyone did."

*I'm afraid I might have to accept the fact that someone out there meant my father harm.*

Dominique's words suddenly shot through his mind

like a bullet and for what seemed like the hundredth time today, the vision of her face swam to the forefront of his thoughts. He missed her. Which didn't make sense. She'd been gone from the palace for four years and he'd gotten accustomed to not seeing her from time to time. Now seven days had passed and he desperately wanted to see her face, hear her voice. But he knew it was best for both of them if he avoided seeing her. So he'd kept to himself and hoped that she was getting on with her life.

"Marcus, I realize you just said you weren't serious. But are you—is there some little part of you that's thinking Father's death might not have been an accident?"

Thankfully, the king's office was very private and no one was around to hear Nicholas's question. Marcus didn't want such rumors to be flying around the castle, or the city for that matter.

"I'd need to read the autopsy report before I could answer that question."

King Nicholas gave him a good-natured grin. "Spoken like a true counselor at work. It's no wonder Father cherished you."

Marcus couldn't imagine anyone cherishing him. Maybe his mother. But she'd worked so hard for most of her life that she'd not had much time to show her love to him. As for Marcus's father, he understood the older man loved him. But he'd often disagreed with Marcus's choices in life and had openly disapproved of his marriage to Liza. And Liza—well, he wasn't sure how his ex-wife had felt about him. He seriously doubted she'd loved him utterly and completely. The way a man and woman are supposed to love each other when they're married. Leaving had been too easy for her.

Pushing the dark thoughts away, he turned his attention back to his new king. "Tell me, Your Highness, how is everyone else in the family feeling about your father's accident now?"

With a long sigh, Nicholas tilted the leather office chair to a more comfortable position. "All of us believe he's most likely dead. Except for Dominique. She refuses to accept he's gone."

Marcus had asked the question in hopes that he would hear a different answer. But he was not surprised. He knew what Dominique was thinking. He was thinking it himself a bit, too. However, he didn't want her to hold on to false hope when there might not be any. It would only hurt her in the end.

"She was very close to King Michael," Marcus reasoned. "Much more so than you and Isabel."

Nicholas smiled wryly. "Well, she is the baby of the family and I guess Father couldn't help but dote on her a little. She seemed to understand him far better than Isabel or myself." His expression suddenly turned anxious and he leaned forward in his chair and looked squarely at Marcus. "Actually, I'm glad the subject of Dominique has come up. I've been very worried about her. All of us have been."

Nicholas's remark jolted Marcus. Far more than it should have. Yet he tried to keep any show of concern from his face as he asked, "Why? What's wrong?"

"Frankly, I don't know. And neither does Isabel. At first we thought it was just grief over losing Father. But now—she doesn't eat enough for a bird. She doesn't leave the castle for any reason. Or have friends over.

She stays cooped up in her rooms and doesn't seem interested in anything. She's pale and listless.''

"What does the Queen think?"

Nicholas shrugged. "You know Mother. She believes all of her children are too strong to crumble. She wouldn't allow it."

"If Dominique is having a health problem, Queen Josephine might not be able to prevent her daughter from crumbling."

Nicholas threw up his hands, then let them fall back to the desktop. "Isabel asked her if she was having a health problem. Dominique nearly bit her head off. Since then Isabel has left her alone. And I can hardly blame her."

Marcus frowned thoughtfully. "That doesn't sound like Dominique."

"No. That's why I'm worried. And I was hoping you might help."

Marcus looked at the other man blankly. "Me? I can't think of any way I could help."

Nicholas shook his head. "She's always thought highly of you, Marcus. And since you're not family, she might talk to you."

Marcus seriously doubted it. They'd not parted on the most comfortable note.

"Have you discussed this with Prudence? The two women are close. Surely she must have a clue about what's going on with her princess."

Nicholas picked up an inkpen and absently began to roll it between his palms. "As a matter of fact, Prudence came to me, worried that Dominique was physically ill."

"Grief can do that to a person," Marcus replied thoughtfully, then with a brief shake of his head, added,

"But I always thought Dominique was stronger than that."

"Now you sound like Mother."

Restlessly, Marcus left his comfortable chair and walked over to the ceiling-to-floor windows. Since he'd entered the office the sun had fallen well below the sea and lights flickered throughout the city and from the boats navigating the river. Yet even though he watched the twinkling colors, he wasn't really seeing their beauty. Only Dominique's.

"I wasn't trying to be blunt, just truthful. Your sister will pick herself up soon, once she's sufficiently grieved over your father." He looked over his shoulder at the other man. "Perhaps you should urge her to go back to the university and finish her studies. It would probably be for the best."

Once again Nicholas tossed up his hands. "Isabel has already tried. Dominique refuses to consider the idea." He paused, then added on a hopeful note, "Prudence thinks you're the only one who can reach her. And I agree. You've always had a special relationship with Dominique. She'll listen to you."

Marcus kept his groan of frustration to himself, yet it was on his face when he turned away from the window and approached the king's desk.

"Just because Dominique had a childish crush on me years ago doesn't mean—"

"Marcus," he quickly interrupted, "Rebecca tells me a woman never entirely forgets her first love. And I know you want what's best for her. Talk to her, please."

Marcus didn't waste his time explaining to King Nicholas that a crush and real love were two different things and that Dominique felt nothing for him now that she'd grown up. King Michael's son was asking for his help and he could hardly refuse. Even though everything inside of him felt it would be a mistake to see Dominique in a private setting.

"All right, Your Highness," he finally acquiesced. "I'll try to find out what's bothering her. But don't be disappointed if my luck isn't any better than Isabel's. Dominique is stubborn and independent like her father."

Smiling now, the king came around from behind the desk and slapped a grateful hand on Marcus's shoulder. "You're right, Marcus. She's more like him than any of us and he'd be mad as hell if we didn't take care of her."

Marcus tried to smile, but it felt as if the muscles in his face were contorted instead. "I'll let you know something once I've spoken to her," he promised.

"Make it tonight, Marcus. And I'll see you tomorrow morning after my meeting with the Swedish ambassador."

In her bedroom, Dominique smoothed her loose dress tightly down against her lower belly and studied the reflection of her silhouette in the cheval mirror. The baby was growing. Even if no one else could see it, she could. If luck was riding with her, she might continue to hide the truth for the next two or three weeks. But already she was about to enter her fourth month; she wasn't going to stay slim and trim much longer.

Dear God, she prayed, what was she going to do? How could she tell her family, especially her mother, that she'd fallen hook, line and sinker for a man who'd wanted nothing more from her than a few nights of sex! It was so shameful and humiliating.

Josephine would sternly point out that she'd not been behaving like a lady. That she'd been thinking with her body and not her head. When in actuality she'd been thinking with neither. Her trusting little heart had gotten her into this mess by leading her to believe she'd loved Bryce and that he'd loved her. But Dominique knew, where her mother was concerned, there would be no excuses for her behavior. Love was not supposed to govern a person's common sense or be put before one's duty to family and country.

With a groan of anguish she turned away from the mirror and headed out of the bedroom. She couldn't keep holding up under this much mental strain. Between her missing father and the coming baby she was beginning to fear her mind was going to snap. She could eat very little and sleep came only in fretful snatches. Several times this past week she'd woken trembling with fear and moist with sweat. Sometimes the nightmares were fuzzy. Others were more clear. In all of them she was either searching for her father or in the terrible throes of labor with no one around to help bring her baby safely into the world.

Desperate to stop her torturous thoughts, Dominique curled up on the end of the couch and turned on the television. She'd never been one to sit idly in front of the screen waiting to be entertained with sitcoms or movies. Normally she didn't need that sort of diversion from everyday life. But lately nothing had been normal for her and tonight, for the first time since she'd been home, Prudence had left her to go on a date.

News. Comedy. Mystery. The doorbell rang just as she was pressing through the channels with blurring speed. The sound startled her, making her drop the remote control at her feet.

Prudence had her own key, she thought. Besides, it was too early for her lady-in-waiting to be back from her date. Isabel was gone for the evening, too, and Nicholas and Rebecca were probably in their own suite having dinner about now.

The buzzer sounded again, longer this time, and Dominique decided she didn't have much choice. She was going to have to answer the caller.

The small foyer leading from the outside door and into the sitting room was small and dimly lit. Even though there was a peephole, Dominique had long ago quit trying to use it to see who was standing on the other side of the door. The guards would not let anyone into the castle without special clearance.

"Who is it?" she called.

"Marcus."

Suddenly she was shaking and she didn't know whether to be glad or mad or to even let him in at all. For the past week, she'd not heard one word from him. She had not seen him anywhere in the castle. He'd been deliberately avoiding her and the knowledge hurt her way too much to be healthy.

"What do you want?" she asked through the door.

"May I come in, Dominique?"

She wanted to ask him why he was bothering to see her now. She wanted to tell him to go away and let her suffer in peace. She wanted to scream at him. But she couldn't afford herself those childish luxuries. Not when she'd made such an issue of being a grown-up woman.

Squaring her shoulders and lifting her chin, she opened the door and stepped back for him to enter. He did so quickly, with little more than a passing glance as he brushed past her and into the small foyer.

Her eyes riveted on his broad back, Dominique shut

the door. Then drawing in a bracing breath, she said coolly, "Please go on into the sitting room. Would you like tea or coffee?"

"Thank you, but I wouldn't want to bother the kitchen help at this late hour," he replied.

She followed him into the sitting room where one small table lamp was burning at the end of the couch. The only other light in the shadowy room was provided by the flickering television screen. Dominique decided to leave things that way. She didn't want Marcus to be able to see her that closely. He might read things from her face. Or he might even notice the small bulge of her stomach. If he did and remarked on it, what would she do or say? she wondered wildly.

Trying not to think of the worst, she took a seat on the couch and motioned for him to take a seat wherever he liked. As he eased his tall frame into a nearby armchair, she noticed tan khakis encased his long legs and a black polo shirt clung loosely to his muscular arms and chest. The casual clothes made him appear more relaxed. More like a man with personal things on his mind rather than political or diplomatic issues. She wondered where she fit in.

"I know I should have called first," he began, "but I was already in the castle and I took the chance that you were home."

She darted her eyes at the television screen rather than continue looking at him. The sight of him was too strong and attractive, too tempting for her frazzled emotions. "I'm surprised you bothered."

"What does that mean?"

Sighing, she ran a hand through her hair. She'd combed it earlier today, but it was messy now, tangling around her head with a mind of its own. But Marcus wasn't here to look at her hair or at her in general. He wasn't motivated by such simple things.

"It means I'm wondering what's brought you here tonight. I know you didn't stop by just for a quick visit. Or you would have done that days ago."

To her horror her voice had developed a quiver and she bit down on her lip, terrified of the tears that usually followed such a warning.

"I've been very busy."

The flimsy excuse was like a douse of petrol on smoldering ashes.

She shot him a mocking look. "I'll bet you practiced that line a lot when you were married. Obviously it didn't work."

Dominique was totally horrified at the words that had just come out of her mouth. She didn't know who had said them. It was like some other woman had taken over her senses.

He didn't say anything and after a moment Dominique shamefully buried her face in her hands. "I'm so sorry, Marcus. That was a horrible thing for me to say. I don't know why I did," she said, her voice muffled and broken by the fingers covering her mouth.

Moments later she felt the weight of his body pressing down on the cushion next to her and then his hand was on her shoulder. Warm, comforting and totally irresistible.

"Dominique," he began softly, "I don't want your apologies. I only want you to tell me what's wrong."

"Nothing is wrong," she said flatly.

"I'm not blind. I can see you're a mess. Talk to me."

His gentle, coaxing voice ripped at the defensive wall she'd thrown between them. "Why?"

"Because I don't want to see you like this."

"You don't want to see me *any* way," she retorted.

He let out a heavy breath and she was acutely aware of his fingers tightening on her shoulder.

"I think you know why I've stayed away," he said solemnly.

Her hands dropped and she lifted her head and stared at him with a mixture of hurt and wonder. "Yes, I believe I do know," she whispered raggedly. "You can't forget that I once had a crush on you. And you're afraid I still want to shower you with that same adoration. The whole idea that I might still care for you is embarrassing. Especially when you look at me—"

Dominique broke off in shock as Marcus took a grip on both her shoulders and gave her a little shake. "Stop it, Dominique! You're talking foolish! You don't know what you're saying!"

The loss and strain she'd been under the past months had seemed to take hold of her, making her reckless and ready to lash out. Especially at him.

"That day at the inn you made it perfectly clear that the idea of you and me together was—was abhorrent to you! Don't try to deny it!"

As he stared at her, his pale eyes took on a strange gleam that Dominique had never seen before, sending a cool shiver rippling down her spine.

"Abhorrent!" he spat angrily. "I was right. You are still a child or you would understand why—" The gleam in his eyes instantly turned to a simmering flame and when he spoke again, his voice was soft and raspy. "Why I can't be near you."

His last words were such a surprise her pink lips formed a silent O, her eyebrows drew together in a furrowed line. "What—"

"What am I talking about? I'm talking about this, Dominique."

Not until he lowered his head toward hers did she realize what he was talking about. And by the time his hard lips had settled over hers, words no longer mattered.

# Chapter Six

Kissing Marcus had often been a fantasy of Dominique's. But this was the real thing and the feelings he was evoking in her couldn't begin to match her imaginings of the past.

She was being sucked into a maelstrom of sensations. She was drowning in the taste of his lips on hers, the feel of his hands sliding beneath her hair and curving around her neck.

Resisting him never entered her mind as she instinctively leaned into him, slid her palms up the solid wall of his chest, then clamped her fingers onto his shoulders.

Marcus reacted to her response by circling his arms around her back and pulling her deeper into his embrace. Her body melted against the heat of his, her lips parted in invitation.

Blood throbbed in his temples as their tongues mated and Dominique's moan of pleasure filled his head. Her lips were soft and giving and sweeter than anything

Marcus had ever tasted. The musky and erotic scent of her skin enveloped his senses and sent his desire sky-rocketing. He didn't want to stop with her lips. He wanted to taste every inch of her. Feel every inch of her with his hands, his mind and his heart.

The shocking thought was like a sobering blast of cold wind and he thrust her away from him even more quickly than he'd begun the embrace.

Stunned and breathless, Dominique stared at him as she pressed two trembling fingers against her swollen lips.

"Marcus?" she whispered.

Regret mingled with the desire still lingering in his eyes and it was all she could do to keep from throwing herself against him and beg him not to stop, to make total and complete love to her.

Raking both hands over his hair, Marcus drew in a ragged breath, but it wasn't enough. He felt as though he'd run a mile at top speed. His heart was still racing madly. Even worse, desire still fired his loins.

This was all wrong, he thought. He wasn't supposed to be wanting this woman. Not this much. And not in this way. But God help him, he did. And he wondered what had happened to his honor and his decency, what it was about Dominique that made him forget everything. Especially who she was and his duty to the Stan-bury family.

With a groan of anguish, he passed a hand over his face, then glanced at her. "Believe me, Dominique, I— that wasn't planned."

She swallowed as emotions tightened her throat. He'd kissed her as though he really wanted her. If he said it meant nothing to him now, it would break what was left of her heart.

"You didn't have to tell me that, Marcus," she said hoarsely.

A long breath drained out of him. "I came here tonight because I was worried about you. Because I wanted to help. But—" He broke off with a groan of self-disgust, then reached for both her hands.

She gave them to him and her heart turned over as his warm fingers tightened intimately around hers. During the four years she'd been gone, Dominique had tried to tell herself that Marcus wasn't her gallant knight. She'd tried to convince herself that he was just a man she'd found overly attractive and after a time he would become no more than a fond acquaintance to her.

When she had met Bryce, she'd believed she'd put Marcus Kent out of her mind completely. But she'd been wrong about Bryce and wrong about Marcus, too. He was her gallant knight and she feared he always would be.

"I know King Michael's disappearance has shattered you, Dominique. I realize you're feeling vulnerable right now and I would never take advantage of that fact," he said, his voice raw but gentle. "Forgive me. Will you?"

Tears sprang to her eyes and she was helpless to stop them. Twin drops rolled down her cheeks as her gaze desperately clung to his. "Oh, Marcus—there's nothing to forgive. I kissed you as much as you kissed me. And—and anyway, I'm—"

She couldn't go on even though the words were clawing at her throat, begging to be released.

His right hand lifted and gently curved around her shoulder. "You're what? Dominique, if I've made you more upset, tell me. I want to help you."

Suddenly everything was too much for her. The touch

of his hand, the tenderness in his eyes, the compassion in his voice. All these weeks she'd been so alone and terrified of an uncertain future. She had to share her fears with this man. She couldn't bear them on her own any longer.

With a little sob of anguish, she flung herself upon him and wept openly against his chest.

Gripped with the need to take away her pain, Marcus held her tightly and murmured soothing words against her ear. His heart ached and he realized what he was feeling for this woman in his arms was something far more than protectiveness.

"It's all right, Dominique. Everything is going to be all right. You're not alone. You're not always going to hurt like this. Losing your father isn't the end of the world."

The last of his words penetrated her tears. She lifted her head and looked at him with frantic need and wretched regret.

"Oh, Marcus, it's not Father. Not entirely. I am sick with grief because he's gone. But there's something else and I don't know what to do—I'm so scared and ashamed and—"

Bewilderment wrinkled his features as he stared down at her. "Ashamed? What have you—"

"I'm pregnant," she blurted before he could finish. "Nearly four months. And my family doesn't know. No one knows. Except you."

If she'd slapped him on both sides of the face he wouldn't have been any more shocked than he was at this moment. She was going to have a child! Some other man had made love to her. The idea ripped through him like a hurtling lance.

"Pregnant! Who—"

She pushed away from him then and swiped the tears from her face with the backs of her hands. "It's a pathetic story, Marcus. I was so stupid. So gullible! I met this graduate student and he seemed to be perfect. He was sweet and attentive and he made me feel special. Not special like royalty. But in a way, well, he believed I was just like any ordinary woman and he picked me just for myself. He had no idea I was a princess."

Marcus grimaced. "Apparently not."

Dominique shook her head. "You don't understand, Marcus. That's one of the major things that drew me to him. I've never wanted to be cared about because I *was* a princess. My mistake was in thinking that Bryce loved me for any reason. He fed me a bunch of sweet lies and I blame myself for not catching on before I let myself be led in by him."

He drew in a long breath as he tried to digest all that she'd just told him. "Didn't any of your friends see what was happening and try to warn you about this man?"

Color seeped into her pale cheeks. "I wish I'd had those sort of close friends at the university. But to be honest, Marcus, I've kept pretty much to myself these past years. Oh, I had friends and acquaintances, but no one I shared deep confidences with. Being a foreigner didn't exactly set me apart, but hiding my real identity did. I felt like I really couldn't open up to people and let them know the real me. But promising to keep my identity a secret was the only way Father would let me attend university in New England. He'd made a private agreement with the president and dean of the college not to reveal my real name to anyone. The only time my real name would be used was when it was written on my degree and even that was to be kept secret. King

Michael didn't want to take the chance that someone might kidnap me for ransom or some way take advantage of my being a princess.''

Marcus grimaced. "I can understand your father's fears. But it looks as though someone managed to take advantage of you in spite of your attending college under an assumed name."

Dominique released a remorseful sigh. "When I met Bryce nothing about my background seemed to matter to him. Ordinary Dominique Danforth was perfect for him. Or so he said."

"Then how do you know Bryce doesn't love you? If the man—"

"He's married, Marcus," she interrupted. "I found out quite by accident, and when I confronted him he didn't bother to deny it. In fact, he even asked me not to make trouble for him and his wife. He admitted that she was expecting a baby soon and his family was important to him. Whereas I, well, it's obvious what I was to him," she finished miserably.

His jaw went tight. For the first time in Marcus's life he felt a murderous urge to track down a man and strangle him with his bare hands. "Then you didn't tell him you were pregnant?"

"No. It was clear I meant nothing to him. He was already married and living with the woman he wanted to be with on a permanent basis. And by then I could see him for what he was and wanted no part of him. Besides, I'm certainly not a home wrecker. I'll let the next vulnerable young woman he seduces tell his wife she's married to a cad."

He breathed a small sigh of relief. "Well, I'm glad you used that much forethought. The idiot deserved trouble. But if you'd tried to dish him a plate of pain it would have only caused you more grief.''

Her head bent, then swung back and forth with regret. "I know you think I'm stupid, Marcus. I know you wouldn't have allowed a woman to dupe you in such a way."

"You're forgetting about Liza," he reminded her dourly.

Surprise lifted her gaze back to his face. "But that was entirely different. Liza married you. She must have loved you in the beginning."

Had she? Marcus wondered. In the beginning of their marriage, she'd often mouthed the words to him. Especially when she was complaining that he didn't spend enough time with her. Now that she'd been gone from his life and he'd had time to look back on their marriage, he suspected her vows of love had been spoken for effect more than anything else. He seriously doubted Liza had ever truly loved him. She'd been impressed with his position and his closeness to the royal family. She'd enjoyed the huge salary he earned and their moments together in bed. But when tragedy had struck, she'd not cared enough to stick by him.

"My divorce was, well, that's over." He shook his head dismissively, then squeezed her shoulder. "The important thing now is your plans."

Her eyes widened at the thought. "I don't know how to tell my family, Marcus. Can't you just imagine the reaction I'm going to get? Especially from Mother."

He nodded grimly. "It won't be easy."

She drew back her shoulders, determined to show him she wasn't going to cave in under the weight. Although there had been times these past few weeks she'd wondered how she could keep going on.

"I'm not expecting anything about it to be easy. But no matter what Mother or anyone says, I love this child. I'm going to have it and raise it myself. Even if I have to leave Edenbourg!"

Marcus glanced at her sharply. He couldn't imagine allowing her to go off alone under such a burden. It was unthinkable. "I don't believe it will come to that, Dominique. Your family loves you. They're not going to desert you."

She bit down on her lower lip. "I'm not so sure, Marcus. I'm going to bring scandal to them all, to the whole country. It's—I'm almost glad Father isn't here to see or hear the gossip this is going to bring down on his family. He'd be so ashamed, so disappointed that I failed him."

Dominique was beating herself up because she'd been human enough to believe a man had loved her. He'd been doing the same thing over Liza, only he hadn't realized it until just this moment.

"Dominique, we all make mistakes. The fact that you're going to have a child doesn't make you any less of a person. Just because your heart was misguided doesn't mean it isn't good."

Tears burned her throat once again, but she held them at bay. Still, the need to feel the rock-solid strength of him had her laying her head against his shoulder and burying her face against his neck.

"I'm so sorry for placing this burden on you, Marcus. Especially now with Father's accident. I'm not your problem and I don't expect you to help me deal with any of it. I'm just going to have to find the courage to tell the family and go on from there. I understand there will be some people in this city and the rest of the country who will say I've tarnished the monarchy. But

I happen to think my baby is more important than gossip.''

His hand lifted to her hair and for long moments he silently stroked the silky strands while his mind raced ahead to the picture she was revealing. He didn't like what he was seeing.

"Dominique, I don't want you to tell your family anything."

Swiftly, she leaned away from him and stared at him in puzzlement. "But—"

"Trust me. Don't say anything. The investigation of your father's accident is still going on and taking up everyone's thoughts. Now isn't the time. And I want to think about what will be best for you and your baby— and the whole family."

She shook her head at him. "What is there to think about, Marcus? The past can't be changed."

He stood, but continued to hold on to her hand. She rose to her feet alongside him.

"Promise me, Dominique. Not a word to anyone until I have time to think what we can do about this."

*We.* He was making it his problem, too. And though she was relieved that she was no longer alone, she couldn't help but wonder why he was bothering. Loyalty to her father was one thing, but helping a pregnant princess was not called for in the duties of king's high counsel.

"All right, Marcus," she agreed with a weary sigh. "I've already kept the secret for this long. I suppose I can manage to keep it to myself a little longer. But I really don't see what difference it will make."

He watched her push back a heavy wave of golden-brown hair. Her fingers were still trembling and except for the two spots of pink on each cheek, her face was white and strained. It frightened him to think losing the baby, or even worse, having a misca that might jeopardize her life. He'd already lost one child and a wife. He couldn't bear to lose Dominique.

Dear Lord, did that mean he was falling in love with her? No, he silently shouted back at himself. He couldn't allow himself to love Dominique. She needed a husband. A father to her child. Someone who would be good at those tasks. Someone who would be worthy of her love. Not a man married to his job.

"Have you seen a doctor, Dominique?"

She nodded uncomfortably. "Yes. Back in the States. To confirm my condition."

"Maybe you should see the royal physician here in the palace," Marcus suggested. "To make sure everything is going along as it should be. You don't have to worry. He'll keep your condition in the most strict confidence."

Dominique looked doubtful. "If the family learns I've had a visit with the doctor they'll surely want to know why."

"I'll tell them I persuaded you to go. Because you've been too upset to sleep. That wouldn't be much of a fib, would it?"

He suddenly smiled and for a moment she wondered what her life would have been like if she'd never gone to New England to attend college. Would Marcus have married and divorced or would she have eventually been able to garner his attention? She didn't know and it was too late to wonder now.

"No. I can't sleep. Or eat for that matter. Prudence thinks I'm coming down with some sort of disease. She's on my case from morning till night."

His hand cupped her cheek and everything inside her went soft and needy.

"I'm going to start badgering you, too. If you don't start taking better care of yourself."

The idea that he cared, even just a little, was enough to make her weepy, but this time the glaze of moisture in her eyes was more from relief than anything.

"I'm so glad you don't hate me," she murmured brokenly.

Something in his eyes went tender and she found her gaze settling on his lips. Knowing the pleasure of his kiss, yet doing without it, was going to be torture, she thought. But then, she was getting used to living with pain. She'd just have to learn to live with a little more of it.

"It would be impossible for me to hate you. For any reason."

His face was only inches away. The roughly hewn planes and angles as familiar as the back of her hand. The urge to lean forward and press her cheek against his was great within her. The desire must have shown on her face because he suddenly cleared his throat and stepped around her.

"Good night, Dominique."

She watched him head toward the foyer and wondered if it was her he didn't trust, or himself.

More than an hour later, Dominique was once again trying to focus her attention on the television, but she was finding it impossible to concentrate on anything.

It still seemed incredible that Marcus had kissed her. Not just a friendly peck on the lips, but a hot, intimate search of her mouth that had sent her senses spinning and her toes curling.

Since he'd left her suite, she'd asked herself again and again why he'd kissed her in such a reckless, all-consuming way. Had his intentions been to simply let her know he was attracted to her physically, even though he didn't want to be?

With a tormented groan, she tried to remember what she'd been saying to prompt such a reaction from him, but she couldn't recall much that had happened before the kiss. Afterward, however, the events were stamped clearly in her mind. The relief she'd felt when she'd told him about the baby was still rushing through her and already lifting some of the depressing weight from her shoulders.

The sound of a key rattling in the door suddenly caught Dominique's attention and she looked up to see Prudence strolling in, her purse and raincoat over her arm, a smile on her face.

"Well, I didn't expect to find you still up," she said cheerfully. "I hope this means you've been out."

Dominique's evening couldn't have been more eventful if she'd flown to Paris and shouted off the Eiffel Tower.

"I've been right here since you left," Dominique informed her.

Prudence made a tsking noise as she carried her things across the room to a coat closet. "You should have had dinner with your family. Gertie made roast beef."

"The maid brought me a plate. I ate some of it," she said, then pushing to her feet, she walked toward one end of the room where a swinging door led into a tiny kitchenette. "Want to join me with a glass of milk?" she called to Prudence.

"You mean you're actually going to put something in your stomach?" Prudence asked.

Dominique wrinkled her nose at the other young woman. Prudence had always been like a sister to her and she regretted being so moody and crabby with her these past days. She only hoped that once her lady-in-waiting learned the truth about her princess, she would forgive Dominique's indiscretions and not judge her too harshly.

"Yes. I'm feeling better this evening."

It was true, she thought, as she pulled a jug of milk from the small refrigerator. For the first time since she'd come home to Edenbourg, she felt as if the world wasn't crumbling around her. Marcus did that to her, she realized. He was more than her gallant protector. More than just a crush or attraction. Even more than a hero. He was the man she loved.

The sudden insight stunned her, like the instant glare of a bright light in a very dark room.

She unconsciously pushed the door on the refrigerator closed, but that was as far as she got to pouring the milk. For long moments her mind continued to whirl. If she told Marcus of her feelings for him, he would never believe her. One kiss and a little time together was not enough to make a person fall in love. He wouldn't understand that while away at college she'd forced her feelings for him to go dormant. But they'd been growing just the same. And all it had taken to bring them back to life was simply seeing him again.

Unaware of the thoughts in her princess's head, Prudence stepped forward and pulled the plastic jug from Dominique's hand. "Here, let me do that. The way you're staring off into space it will be midnight before you get the milk poured."

A soft blush stole over Dominique's cheeks as she shook her head and forced her attention back to Prudence. "I'm sorry. I was just thinking about something."

"Clearly," Prudence replied as she took down glasses from a cabinet. "Is it your father? Have you heard anything new about the accident?"

"No," she answered quickly, then glanced at Prudence as the other woman poured the milk. "How did your evening go?"

Prudence rolled her eyes. "Boring. For the past two hours I've been listening to stories about a fishing trip, a soccer game and the joys of selling life insurance."

Dominique smiled with amusement as she took the offered glass from Prudence's hand. "Where did you meet this guy anyway?"

"At the business school I attended while you were away at college. I only agreed to go out with him because I didn't want to hurt his feelings."

"Better now than later."

Prudence nodded wholeheartedly. "Believe me, the next time he calls I'm going to be conveniently busy."

Dominique sipped the milk and was relieved her stomach actually welcomed the nourishment.

"I had company tonight," she said.

"Really?" Prudence looked both surprised and pleased at this news. "Who was it? Your sister?"

Dominique shook her head and for some reason the corners of her lips wanted to curve up into a silly grin. But she tamped down the urge. A smile coupled with Marcus's name would send Prudence's imagination into overdrive.

"No. It was Marcus Kent."

Prudence's eyebrows shot up. "Oh. What was he doing? Discussing your father's accident?"

"Actually, we didn't get around to that topic."

Dominique could virtually see the wheels inside the other woman's head spinning. "I thought that subject was at the top of everyone's conversation these past couple of weeks. So, what *did* you two talk about?"

Talking had not been the highlight of the evening. But Dominique could hardly tell Prudence about the kiss. The intimate embrace she'd shared with Marcus was too private, too precious to divulge to anyone, including her lady-in-waiting.

Her gaze drifted to the floor rather than remain on Prudence's inquisitive face. "Nothing in particular. He merely came by to see how I've been doing."

"Oh. Just a dutiful family call, I guess."

"Probably. Marcus does take his duties seriously."

She could feel Prudence regarding her thoughtfully. "I'm beginning to see that," she said dryly.

Dominique shot her an annoyed frown. "If you're thinking Marcus has romantic intentions toward me, you're dead wrong, Prudence. The man has been married and divorced. He doesn't want another woman in his life!"

Prudence's response was a knowing smile that had Dominique heaving a sigh of irritation.

"What are you smiling about?" Dominique hurled the question at her. "Do you think that's funny?"

The suggestive grin remained on Pru's face. "No. I think it's rather telling that ever since you returned from your outing with Marcus last week, you've been moping. And now that you've seen him again, you've come back to life. I admit you've been grieving for your father, but that's not your real problem. You're in love with Marcus Kent!"

# Chapter Seven

The next afternoon, Dominique was on her way down to the courtyard to take a walk in the garden when she rounded a bend in the stairwell and nearly bumped head on into Marcus.

"Dominique!"

Grabbing a hold on her elbow, he steadied her teetering weight. "I'm surprised to find you here in this part of the castle," he said, his gaze quickly traveling down her loose yellow sweater and slim beige capri pants. "Are you going out somewhere?"

She smiled faintly and wondered if, like her, he'd spent most of the night thinking about their kiss. No, he was too mature, she mentally argued. He was a man and they didn't romanticize, they simply enjoyed what they were doing at the moment, then later forgot about it entirely.

"Only to the gardens for a walk," she answered. "I took this long route through the castle to get more exercise."

His hand still on her arm, he moved up to the step where she was standing. The nearness of him shook her and she tried not to notice how tall and commanding he looked in his dark suit or the way his gold-brown eyes slid leisurely over her face.

"You look better today. There's color in your cheeks."

She could have told him the color in her cheeks was there because she felt self-conscious. After Prudence had taken one look at her last night and decided she was in love with Marcus, Dominique feared anyone and everyone might see beneath her skin and know what she was really feeling.

Before she'd retired to bed last night, she'd argued loud and long with Prudence, denying the other woman's accusation. But now as she looked at Marcus's strong, handsome face, she was melting with the need to touch him again, to feel his breath upon her cheek, to experience the erotic magic of his lips.

She breathed deeply and nervously reached up to touch the brown scarf she'd twisted, then tied around her long hair. "Thank you. I feel somewhat better."

Marcus glanced cautiously behind them, then back down the stairwell as if to make sure the two of them were completely alone.

"I'm glad I've run into you like this," he said. "I was intending to call you as soon as I got back to my office."

Her heart began to thump with foolish anticipation. "Oh. Why?"

"I want you to have dinner with me tonight."

Have dinner with Marcus? The two of them had gotten vexed with each other while having a simple drink at the inn. A whole dinner might be even worse, she considered. And how could she possibly sit across from him for any length of time and not say, *Marcus, I love you. I've loved you for a long time. Only I've just now realized it.*

"Do you think that's wise, Marcus?" she asked, then seeing the frown on his face, she quickly went on, "I mean, everyone is soon going to know I'm pregnant. You don't want your good name to be sullied, too."

He frowned at her. "You let me worry about my name. Right now, I want to hear you say you're agreeable to having dinner with me tonight. There's something I want to talk over with you. And we both have to eat anyway."

In other words, he was making it clear there would be nothing romantic about the evening. The whole thing would be strictly business for him. Which wasn't surprising to Dominique. One kiss from Marcus Kent didn't equal romance. It didn't equal anything. So if she planned to keep her sanity, she was going to have to forget last night once and for all.

She sighed. "What time shall I be ready?"

He pushed back his cuff and studied a slim silver wristwatch. "I still have two more meetings before I quit for the day. I'll come fetch you from your suite around seven. Will that be okay?"

Where she and Marcus was concerned, nothing was okay. But she had to pretend it was. She had to keep on pretending he was a friend who was simply trying to help her. Nothing more.

"I'll be ready," she promised.

His gaze slid slowly, appreciatively over her face. "Good."

A footstep sounded from the stairwell higher above

them. Marcus instantly dropped his hold on her arm and stepped away from her side just as Luke Stanbury came into view.

The sight of Dominique and Marcus stopped him short, as though he'd not been expecting to find anyone in this lonely end of the castle. But he collected himself quickly and a bright smile instantly appeared on his face.

"Well, hello," he said to the two of them, then added with a chuckle. "I'm glad to see I'm not on a dead end and that people really do use this part of the castle."

Dominique smiled at her cousin. "Don't worry, Luke. Most people who aren't accustomed to the castle's endless stairs and hallways easily get lost in all the twists and turns."

"Were you headed somewhere in particular?" Marcus asked him.

The cool tone of Marcus's question surprised Dominique, but Luke didn't seem to notice. He continued to regard both of them with a friendly smile.

"Down to the courtyard. To the gardens. Aunt Josephine tells me that a few of the flowers are starting to bloom now, so I thought I'd go have a look."

"What a coincidence," Dominique told him amiably. "I was just going there myself. If you'd like to join me, I'll show you the way."

The tall, dark-headed American stepped down eagerly and looped his arm through Dominique's. "I'd be delighted. It's not every day a man gets to be escorted by a beautiful princess."

Dominique glanced pointedly at Marcus. "I'll see you later."

His only acknowledgment was a nod of his head, but as the two of them walked past him and on down the stairwell, Dominique could feel his gaze following her and Luke. She wondered what Marcus was thinking about. Her, or her American cousin?

Later that evening, Dominique was in her bedroom dressing for her approaching dinner with Marcus when she heard voices in the outer room. Moments later, a knock sounded on the doorjamb and she glanced away from the mirror to see her sister standing in the open doorway. Like their brother, Isabel was tall with dark hair. She'd always been an independent, take-charge sort of person. Dominique had always admired her and looked up to her. And she desperately hoped when Isabel found out about the coming baby, she wouldn't condemn her.

"Well, don't you look pretty!" she exclaimed.

Dominique glanced down at the dress she'd chosen to wear. It was a loosely fitted sheath that stopped just at the top of her knees. The outer layer was concocted of sheer chiffon splashed with pale pink roses. Beneath the overlay of flowers, a darker dusky pink crepe clung more closely to the curves of her body.

"Thank you," she said, then gestured nervously to her dress. "You don't think this is a bit too much for a casual dinner, do you?" She looked up, giving her sister a helpless smile. "I've never had your sense of taste."

Scoffing at Dominique's words with a wave of her hand, Isabel stepped into the room. "You look perfect. And I'd say your tastes are extremely good," she added with a smile. "Prudence tells me you have a dinner date with Marcus."

Dominique groaned. "Prudence has a loose tongue. It's hardly a dinner date! We're just friends."

"Well, whatever it is, I'm glad you're getting out of this suite. That's the reason I'm here, actually," Isabel explained. "To force you to have dinner with the family tonight. But you already have something much better to do. So I'm going to leave and let you finish getting ready."

Isabel started out of the room and Dominique turned back to her reflection in the mirror. Then before her sister could step through the door, she called to her.

"Isabel, do you think I should wear my hair up? Like this?" Hurriedly, she twisted the heavy tresses into the semblance of a French twist at the back of her head.

Tilting her head to one side, Isabel studied her thoughtfully from one angle, then another. Eventually, she shook her head. "Leave it down. The twist is pretty, but it makes you look older."

With a little wave of her hand, Isabel left the bedroom.

Smiling to herself, Dominique reached for a box of hairpins and went to work pinning up her golden-brown mane.

Marcus called for her promptly at seven and declined to have a drink before they left Dominique's suite.

"Dinner is all ready and waiting for us," he explained. With a hand at her back, he guided her across a wide corridor and to the first stairwell that would lead them down to the palace grounds.

"Is your car parked in the courtyard?" Dominique asked as they descended the curving stone steps.

"No. I didn't bring the car around. I thought we'd walk. Will your shawl be enough wrap?"

She glanced at him with comiclike confusion. "You mean we're going to walk all the way into town?"

He chuckled. "No. I thought I explained. Maybe I didn't. Luke interrupted us and I guess I didn't have the chance to tell you we'd be having dinner at my apartment."

His apartment! All along she'd pictured them going to one of the more elite restaurants in Old Stanbury. She'd certainly not imagined anything so...private. Dear Lord, how was she going to keep her mind off him without anyone around to distract her. Especially with the way he looked tonight in a crisp white shirt, gray paisley tie and charcoal-colored trousers. His jet-black hair was brushed back from his face and, even in the darkness, glistened like a raven's wing.

"Oh," she murmured. "I didn't realize."

He glanced down at her at the same time he took a light hold on her arm. He'd never seen her looking more beautiful, he realized. The glow of her smooth, creamy skin was enhanced by the pink color of her dress. The upsweep of her hair revealed her long, slender neck. A single emerald nestled in the hollow of her throat and dangled from her earlobes. With each step they took across the palace grounds toward his apartment, he wondered how he was going to keep his hands off her.

"That is agreeable with you, isn't it?" he asked, half hoping she would demand he take her somewhere more public. Someplace he wouldn't be tempted to make love to her. But Marcus wasn't sure there was such a place. Just looking at Dominique strained his self-control. "I wanted us to have our privacy. But we could drive into town if you'd prefer."

Anticipation slithered down her spine, but whether it was from his touch or his words, Dominique wasn't sure. The one thing she did know was that she was definitely going to have to keep a firm grip on herself tonight. Or Marcus was going to read her like an open book with full illustrations.

"Of course your apartment is fine," she told him. "But I was expecting us to go somewhere more public."

By now they had descended to the bottom floor of the castle. Marcus opened a heavy wooden door bearing the Stanbury crest and Dominique proceeded him outside of the building.

Before King Michael's accident there would have been only one royal guard standing duty outside the castle exit. But minutes after the family had been alerted of the car crash, Marcus had advised Nicholas to increase security twofold. At least until it was proven that the accident was just an accident and nothing more. Therefore, tonight there were two guards to watch the comings and goings of this particular castle door.

Nicholas and the whole family still considered Marcus's order a bit overprotective. In their opinion, the king had died in an automobile crash. There was no reason to suspect that any of the Stanburys were in jeopardy from outside forces. But as for Dominique, the sight of the extra guards was welcomed anyway.

Behind her, Marcus watched one of the guards close the door, then returning his hold on her arm, he began to guide her down a stone walkway. Both sides were bordered with carefully sculpted waist-high hedgerows and lit with softly glowing footlights. The night was clear. Stars twinkled in the inky sky while far to the east a crescent moon hung out over the sea.

Her sigh was silent as his arm slipped around the back of her waist.

"I apologize, Dominique. You must have been looking forward to dinner at a nice restaurant. But what I have to say to you can't be said in public.''

His comment left her wordless and the two of them walked the remaining distance to his apartment in silence.

A few minutes later, inside Marcus's cozy living room, Dominique handed him her chiffon shawl and gazed around her with open interest.

"Is this where you lived while you and Liza were married?'' she asked frankly.

"No,'' he answered. "We had a bigger apartment in town.''

She was glad Liza hadn't lived within these walls, she realized. The knowledge of another woman sharing this small home with Marcus would have made her uncomfortable. Probably even jealous. Though she had no right to be.

He put her light wrap away in a small nearby closet, then came back to where she was standing in the middle of the room.

"Would you like to have a drink before we eat?'' he asked.

The apartment was very quiet. So quiet that Dominique could hear the old German clock on the wall ticking with each swing of the pendulum and the crackle of the burning logs in the fireplace.

"A drink isn't necessary,'' she answered. "Because of the baby I've forgone spirits, so it would have to be juice or milk anyway. But if you'd like a cocktail, please, go ahead.'' She glanced curiously toward an open doorway that she suspected would lead into the kitchen. "Is there—do you have help waiting to serve us?''

He grinned at her question. "I'm our waiter tonight.

I do have a cook and maid, but I let them go earlier this evening.''

When he'd said private, he'd meant private in every sense of the word, Dominique thought. Apparently he didn't want anyone overhearing them discuss her father's accident or the coming baby.

Her faint laugh was full of disbelief as she gazed pointedly around at the walls and floors. ''Do you think we should check the place for wires or bugs of some sort?''

Marcus couldn't scold her for making light of the situation. It was the first time he'd heard her laugh in a long time and the sound filled him with unexplained pleasure. Last night, when she'd sobbed openly in his arms, he'd felt his own heart break. He wanted her to be happy. He wanted that more than he had ever wanted anything for himself.

''I've had the whole place swept for electronical devices,'' he teased. ''So I can safely say we can eat in the dining room or in here by the fire. Take your pick.''

She glanced at the cheerful fire and the glow of pleasure in her green eyes gave Marcus his answer. He led her over to a small square table and two chairs positioned to one side of the brick hearth.

''You sit and I'll bring everything in,'' he said as he helped her into one of the padded wooden chairs.

Dominique's soft chuckle drifted up to him and he smiled in spite of everything that was on his mind.

''Marcus, I've always thought of you as a government official, not a waiter.''

''I have a few hidden talents,'' he said jokingly, ''but don't worry—I didn't do the cooking.''

Moments later, he pushed in a cart loaded with everything they needed for their dinner. Crisp coleslaw, grilled snapper, baby sweet peas in white sauce, scalloped potatoes and thick buttered slices of sourdough bread.

For once Dominique's worries had left her appetite alone and she ate with hungry pleasure. Across the table, Marcus enjoyed watching her eat more than he enjoyed the food on his own plate.

"I don't suppose you heard anything new from the police today?" she asked once they'd gotten well into the meal.

"I talked with the chief investigator this morning. The autopsy on the king's driver is still ongoing. The authorities want to make sure no stone is left unturned. Every possible test is being done on Herbert's remains."

"I realize I need to have more patience," she conceded as she cut into a bite of flaky fish. "But not knowing about my father's body, or about the whole accident, is so frustrating."

He nodded. "How was your walk with Luke this afternoon?"

She shrugged. "He's outwardly charming. But—"

"On the inside?"

She gave him a helpless smile. "I can't really say. He only stayed in the garden about five minutes. And then he suddenly remembered he had something to do and headed back into the castle. So I really didn't exchange that much conversation with the man. But from what little I have, he seems nice enough. So do Jake and Uncle Edward."

He sighed. "Yes, all three appear to be genuinely fond of your mother and she of them. But I still can't forget the timing of their arrival in Old Stanbury. It doesn't sit right with me."

Dominique agreed with Marcus. The chance of estranged relatives arriving at the same time as her father's accident merely out of coincidence seemed incredible. Yet so far none of the American Stanburys had behaved out of line or suspiciously in any way. In fact, all three seemed quite eager to help with the investigation.

"Did Father ever mention Uncle Edward to you?" she asked Marcus thoughtfully.

"Now and then. I think it weighed on him that the two of them didn't get along. King Michael considered his brother a wastrel, but I still got the impression that he loved him in spite of his failings."

"You could be right," Dominique said. "But that doesn't sound like Father. He always expected high standards from his family. Especially from his children." She shook her head regretfully and reached for her water glass. "Like I said last night, I'm almost glad he can't see me now."

When she placed the glass back down beside her plate, Marcus reached across the table and touched her hand. "Dominique, you and the baby are the main reason I wanted to talk to you privately tonight. Not about your father's accident."

She took a deep breath and let it out. "Marcus, last night, well, it was wonderful of you to say you would help me. But frankly, there's nothing you can do. Except maybe stand behind me when I do tell the family."

He glanced at her plate, which was nearly empty. "Are you finished? Would you like dessert?"

She shook her head. "I couldn't eat another bite. But a cup of decaffeinated coffee with a little cream would be nice."

He came around the table and helped her up from the chair.

"I'll go get the coffee and we'll have it on the couch," he told her.

"Let me help you," she offered.

"No. You make yourself comfortable," he said. "I'll be right back."

He left the room and Dominique went over to a dark leather couch positioned directly in front of the small fireplace, a few feet away from the hearth. March nights were usually still cool in Edenbourg and tonight was no exception. The heat of the flames felt good against her bare arms and legs.

She settled into the buttery soft cushion and closed her eyes. How wonderful it would be, she mused, to be cocooned safely away with Marcus. A place where the horror of King Michael's accident or the scandal of her condition didn't exist. Here in his apartment, she felt more at ease than she had in a long time. Marcus had that steadying effect on her. But she realized even Marcus couldn't stop the disgrace she would soon be facing.

"Dominique? Are you feeling all right?"

Her eyes shot open to see Marcus standing over her with a cup and saucer in his hand, his expression full of concern.

She quickly scooted to the edge of the cushion and accepted the coffee from him. "I'm sorry, Marcus. I was just relaxing. It's so quiet and comfortable here."

With his own cup in hand, he eased down carefully beside her. "My apartment is a far cry from your suite of rooms in the castle," he pointed out.

She smiled with bland acceptance. "Yes. The castle is elaborate. But simple feels good to me."

"Back in the States you lived in an apartment on campus, didn't you?"

With a nod, she said, "At first it was quite a change from the austerity of the palace. But I quickly learned to love the hominess, the complete privacy I had in my little rooms."

His gold-brown eyes thoughtfully studied her face. "Then you liked the anonymity of living there and going to school under an assumed name."

After a careful sip of hot coffee, she said, "I loved the sense of freedom it gave me. But I didn't like keeping a part of who I really was hidden from everyone. Holding back the fact that I was a princess of Edenbourg always made me feel, well, like a bit of an outsider. And now I have this other secret about the baby," she went on helplessly. "It seems like I'm doomed to keep living with some sort of deception. And frankly, Marcus, it's wearing me down."

"I'd already gathered that impression from you last night."

Her wan smile was full of resignation. "What is that old saying? We have to lie in the bed we make for ourselves? Well, I'm tired of sitting on the side of the mattress. I'm ready to lie down and take what's coming to me. Whether that be good or bad."

She was a brave soul, Marcus thought. Another woman in her position would have probably already crumbled under the strain. Liza's foundation had certainly cracked and she'd had a giant circle of family and friends around to support her through tragedy. So far Dominique had been facing her personal crisis all alone. He admired her strength and he was more determined than ever to see that no harmful thoughts or words were ever flung her way. She didn't deserve them.

He cleared his throat, then placed his cup and saucer on the low table in front of them. "I've been thinking about this whole thing with you and the baby, Dominique, and I believe I've come up with the perfect solution."

Her eyes widened with interest as he turned to face her. "I can't imagine any solution being perfect for this situation I'm in. But please, tell me anyway."

His gaze settled on her lovely face and he felt a strange pressure begin to fill his chest.

"I want you to marry me, Dominique. I haven't forgotten that you are a member of the royal family and I'm only a commoner...but I believe your immediate problem supercedes all that. I want you to become my wife."

# Chapter Eight

"**M**arried!" One hand lifted to a spot between her breasts. She wasn't sure if her lungs were going to continue working. She couldn't seem to get a breath in or out. "Did I hear you correctly, Marcus?"

He could see that he had stunned her. Last night, when he'd made the decision to propose to her, he'd stunned himself. Yet he was more certain than ever that a marriage between them was the right thing to do. For her and himself.

"You heard right."

Mindlessly, she placed her cup and saucer on the low table alongside his.

"I—you've knocked the wind from me, Marcus. I—really don't know what to say."

He smiled wryly. "When a woman is proposed to, she's supposed to say yes," he told her.

A breathless laugh rushed past her lips. "But that's when the proposal is—is traditional and the man doing the proposing is the right man."

His eyes narrowed to a guarded expression. "Are you saying I'm not the right man for you?"

Oh Lord, he was the perfect man for her. Somehow she'd even understood that four years ago. She had even dreamed of how it might be to have Marcus propose to her. But that had only been the wishful dreams of a young woman in the first throes of budding love. She was older and wiser now. She knew there was nothing romantic about this proposal. And the very fact tore at her tender heart.

"Marcus—this is—don't be silly. You're a wonderful man. The best. But that doesn't mean—"

Troubled by his watchful gaze, she rose from the couch and walked over to the fireplace. To her dismay he followed and took her gently by the shoulders. The warmth of his hovering body overwhelmed the heat of the flames.

"Dominique," he began, "you know that I'm not the sort of man who would ever say something of this magnitude if I didn't truly mean it."

"Yes. I do realize that you are serious. I just don't understand—"

She broke off, her mind whirling with all sorts of implications. Why would Marcus offer to do such a thing for her? she wondered wildly. He was a dutiful man. But this was something entirely different. Had he stopped to consider what this would do to his job, his life?

"It's very easy to understand, Dominique. You are not just a pregnant young woman without a husband. You are a princess of Edenbourg. And though I don't have royal blood running through my veins, I want to give you the shelter of my name and acknowledge that the child you are carrying is mine. The idea of you marrying a commoner for love would be accepted by the public much more readily than if they discovered you were an unwed mother.''

She sucked in another shocked breath. "You—you would tell everyone that you fathered the baby?"

He nodded solemnly and she immediately began to swing her head back and forth.

"Marcus, such an admission from you would ruin your reputation, your credibility as king's high counsel!"

"A divorce didn't ruin it," he reasoned. "And becoming a father is a much more honorable thing in the public's eyes. In my eyes, too," he added.

He was serious. A part of her wanted to dance and shout with happiness. The man she loved wanted her to be his wife. Yet her heart knew it wasn't right for her. She needed and wanted more from him than his upright name and the protection it would lend her.

"I wasn't expecting anything like this from you, Marcus," she murmured, her gaze sliding from his eyes to the faint cleft in his strong chin.

"Clearly."

The need to touch him became too great to resist and she rested her palms against his chest. She could feel the thud, thud of his heart and the human drumbeat seduced her senses in much the same way as his smile and the stroke of his fingers did along her skin.

"I don't know what to say, Marcus."

The corners of his mouth tilted upward and then one hand lifted to gently cup the side of her face. It was all Dominique could do to keep from closing her eyes and leaning into him.

"I believe the word is yes," he whispered.

Three little letters connected together. So simple to

say, she thought. But later, would she find it simple to live with a man whom she knew didn't love her?

Anguished by the picture in her head, she turned her back to him and drew in a ragged breath. "I can't give you a definite answer tonight, Marcus. This is too important a decision to be making on the spur of the moment."

She sensed him moving closer and then his fingers were on the back of her neck, sliding intimately against the tender skin exposed by her upswept hair.

"I'm sure I don't need to remind you that time is important. If we're going to tell the public that I'm the father of your child, I don't want you to be so pregnant that they'll get the idea I had to be dragged to the altar."

Longing of a kind she'd never felt coiled in the pit of her stomach. "That's another thing, Marcus. Except for coming home to Stanbury castle on the holidays, I've been living in the States. A baby can't be made at that distance."

But it certainly could at this distance, she thought. The front of Marcus's body had moved closer and was now pressed lightly against hers. And when he spoke his voice was a seduction all its own.

"You were home for nearly two weeks this past Christmas," he pointed out. "That's ample time for us to have conceived a child together. And the timing would be just about perfect. Love at Christmas—a baby in September."

She groaned mentally at the picture he was painting. A love affair with Marcus! Many times when she was younger, she'd imagined herself in such a situation. Now he was asking her to pretend such a thing had really happened. It was all so ironic she didn't know whether she wanted to laugh or cry.

"We didn't really see each other at Christmas holiday. But no one really knows that. And the timing would work," she meekly agreed as she found herself wanting to give in to the temptation of becoming Marcus Kent's wife. But a marriage under such conditions would never work. She couldn't allow him to seduce her into the notion.

Quickly, before he made her lose all resistance, she stepped away from him. With her back still to him, she clasped her hands together in prayerful need.

"I'll—I'll think about it, Marcus. And give you a definite answer…soon. Now if you don't mind, I'd like to go back to the castle. I'm really rather wrung-out."

"I'll drive you back in the car."

She turned to see him fetching her shawl from the closet. "No. Don't bother with the car. I can walk. I'm not that exhausted."

He wrapped the thin piece of material around her upper shoulders. Dominique's heartbeat sped up madly as his hands hovered just above her breasts.

"I'll walk back with you."

Without looking up at him, she nodded.

He sighed. "Are you angry with me? Again?"

She lifted her gaze to his and tried to smile, but the muscles in her face refused to display what her heart wasn't feeling.

Touching her hand to his cheek, she said, "I've never been angry with you, Marcus."

*Only in love with you. Now and forever.*

"Dominique, what is the matter with you? Other than Marcus Kent?"

From her seat on the balcony, Dominique glanced

around to see her lady-in-waiting bearing down on her with a look of determination.

"Please, Pru, I don't want to have this discussion today," she said wearily.

"Who said anything about a discussion?" she retorted with an airy wave of her hand. "I came out here to drag you out of that chair. You've been sitting in the same spot for nearly two hours."

"I've been enjoying the sun. It's a beautiful day," she reasoned.

"So it is," Prudence agreed. "But there's no book in your lap so you cannot even bother pretending to be reading. Each time I've glanced out here, the only thing I see you doing is sitting and brooding the afternoon away."

Dominique frowned at her. "I haven't been brooding. I've been thinking. There's a difference, you know."

"Deep concentration coupled with a dour frown equals brooding in my dictionary."

Dominique wasn't sure what she'd been doing these past few hours or the past week for that matter. Since the night she'd had dinner with Marcus, her every waking moment was spent thinking about his proposal.

He was waiting for her answer. All she had to do was say yes and the immediate problem of her advancing pregnancy would be solved. It would be simple, yet she knew marrying Marcus wouldn't be right. Not when he didn't love her. The marriage would be an imitation and the pretense would end up breaking her heart.

"Oh, Pru, you're worse than a mother hen," Dominique said crossly. "Ever since I've come home for LeAnn's christening you've accused me of not being myself. Well, there's plenty of reasons—"

Her words stopped as both women caught the sound

of the telephone ringing from inside Dominique's bedroom.

"I'll get it," Prudence told her and hurried away to put a stop to the shrill noise.

Dominique rose from her chair and stretched. She had been sitting too long. She needed to go for a walk and clear her head. Most of all, she needed to see Marcus and put an end to his marriage plan once and for all.

With that thought in mind, she turned to head back into the castle and met Prudence rushing toward her.

"Dominique, that was King Nicholas on the phone," she quickly explained. "He wants you to meet with the rest of the family in the sitting room."

"When?" Dominique asked with mild interest.

"Immediately."

She frowned. "What's the rush? Did he explain—"

"No," Prudence interrupted. "But I could tell from his voice that something serious must be going on. He sounded grim."

Dominique felt a sinking feeling deep inside her and she sent up a swift, silent prayer. "It's Father. They've heard something about King Michael!"

She hurried past Prudence and into her bedroom. After jerking a brush through her long hair, she pushed her feet into a pair of black ballerina slippers. The full gauze skirt and cropped sweater she was wearing were far too casual for a family meeting, but she didn't care. If this was news about her father she couldn't hear it soon enough.

Prudence left the suite with her and after a fairly mad dash to another wing of the castle, the two women found the family room already crowded.

Immediately Dominique's gaze zeroed in on Marcus, who was standing next to Nicholas at the head of the room, near the huge stone fireplace. Their dark heads were together, their expressions stern as they talked to each other and no one else.

Rebecca, baby LeAnn and Isabel, along with her lady-in-waiting, Rowena Wilde, were all seated on a nearby couch and all, except the baby, looked anxious. Josephine was in her armchair. Her dress was crisp, the raspberry color a perfect foil against her brown hair, which was twisted into its usual chignon. The expression on her face was smooth, as though nothing dreadful was about to be announced. But then Dominique knew she couldn't gauge her mother's behavior against the average person's.

Across the room, Edward Stanbury was standing next to a floor-length window, his attention turned toward the view of the city. Nearby, Luke and Jake were sharing a brocade-covered settee. Jake's young son, Sammy, was perched on his father's knee. At the moment the child was quietly preoccupied with a small toy in his hands.

Dominique took a seat in a vacant armchair near her mother. Prudence went to join the other women on the couch.

"Mother, what is this about?" Dominique asked in a lowered voice. "I've never seen Nicholas look so severe."

Josephine gave her daughter a small smile. "I don't know, my dear. Your brother has so far only spoken with Marcus, and I have no idea what the two men are discussing."

Dominique started to ask her mother another question, but stopped as she noticed Marcus leaving her brother's side and walking straight toward her.

Without a word, he took a seat on the arm of her

chair, then reached for her hand. Careful to keep the surprise from her face, she gave it to him. While inside she wondered what was motivating this sudden display of public affection. For as long as she'd known him, he'd never done such a blatant thing. She could only conclude that he was setting up a picture for their future wedding announcement. The thought made her feel even worse.

"Marcus, why are we here?" she asked him. "Is this something about Father?"

His fingers tightened on hers. "I think you should hear this from Nicholas. He'll explain everything."

She looked at her brother just as he stepped to the center of the massive stone hearth. Instantly the voices around the room hushed and the hysterical thought ran through Dominique that this whole meeting was like a theatrical event. The lights were dimming and the curtains opening upon the first act. Her brother was acting as king of Edenbourg. Only this wasn't a play. And the remaining cast and crew knew nothing of the plot.

"My dear family and friends," he began soberly, "I've called you all here this afternoon so that everyone will be privy to the news that was given to me only minutes ago.

"As everyone is aware," he went on, "the investigators have been waiting for the complete results of the autopsy performed on Herbert, King Michael's beloved driver. This afternoon the results have been handed to me. And to be frank, they are—quite shocking."

Dominique glanced fearfully up at Marcus. He shook his head ever so slightly and tightened his hold on her hand.

"Do go on, Nicholas," Josephine urged. "Don't keep us waiting."

Dominique's gaze swung over to her mother. In spite of her placid expression, she could tell Josephine was anxious. Faint color tinged her cheeks and her jeweled hand gripped the arm of her chair.

In the past weeks since King Michael's disappearance, Dominique had longed to see some sort of grief or distress from her mother. Some sign that the queen cared that her king was gone. But now that Dominique had witnessed it firsthand, it only made her feel the loss of her father even more.

Nicholas cleared his throat, then glanced around the room at each and every face.

"The results," he finally spoke, "show that Herbert was murdered. He was dead before the car crashed and burned on the cliff."

"Murdered! My Lord," Isabel cried out. "How?"

"A lethal dose of digitalis," Nicholas answered his sister's question.

Everyone in the room began to talk wildly and all at once. Queen Josephine quickly clapped her hands and demanded silence.

When quietness fell, she said, "Nicholas, I'm not sure finding digitalis in Herbert's blood could be viewed as murder. The man had a heart condition. He took digitalis to control it. He could have simply taken an extra dose by mistake."

Nicholas shook his head. "No, Mother. The forensic examiners were aware of Herbert's medical treatment. This wasn't an innocent, accidental overdose. There was a massive amount of this drug in Herbert's system. The coroner believes he was probably injected with it, though the burned condition of his body made the exact source of ingestion impossible to determine. In any case, there was no smoke inhalation in his lungs from the fire, so it is clear he was dead before the crash."

"That's ghastly!" Edward practically shouted from across the room. "Who would want to do such a thing to my brother's driver?"

Once again, Dominique turned her face up to Marcus. "If Herbert was murdered, what about Father?" she whispered to him. "Do the police think—"

Her brother's voice interrupted her question and she paused to listen with the rest.

"The investigators believe King Michael has been kidnapped," Nicholas continued. "If he'd been murdered along with Herbert, his body would have more than likely been discovered nearby. But as we all know, that didn't happen."

"Kidnapping doesn't make sense," Josephine said, her features drawn. "There has been no contact. No demand for ransom."

"That's right," Isabel inserted. "Why kidnap a king and not ask for money?"

"Police investigators believe the motive, when they learn it, will be the link to solving this whole incident," Nicholas explained.

"Perhaps someone, an enemy of this country, wants to take power of the throne?" Luke suggested.

Marcus looked at the other man, then spoke for the first time since Nicholas had given them all the shocking news.

"Killing a king doesn't leave his throne open for just any outsider to take over. His heirs are next in power. The enemy would have to extinguish the whole Stanbury family to overtake the throne."

"Unless the enemy *was* a Stanbury," Edward said soberly.

Every head in the room turned to Michael Stanbury's brother as the tall, gray-haired man moved away from the window and stepped to the center of the room.

Nicholas glared at his uncle. "What are you trying to say, Edward? That one of *us* did away with Father?" he demanded.

"You were his heir and the first in line to the throne," Edward casually pointed out. "You've now become the king."

"Edward! Nicholas loved his father!" Josephine admonished with enough heat to scorch every soul in the room.

Instantly, Edward rounded Josephine's chair, then kneeling in front of her, he took hold of both her hands. "I'm sorry, my dear sister-in-law," he said with seemingly genuine sincerity. "I wasn't trying to accuse Nicholas of anything. I was merely pointing out what the public is probably going to be thinking when the news of the autopsy reaches the papers and television."

His features hard, Nicholas said, "I believe the public is going to be thinking a number of things. And yes, one of them will probably be that I wanted to be king of this country so badly that I did away with my own father rather than wait for his natural death. But I also have the feeling that many will be discussing the Stanbury Chamber of Riches and what part it might be playing in this whole grisly incident."

Edward straightened away from Josephine, but still stood close to her side. Dominique got the odd impression that the older man truly did care for his sister-in-law. But then she'd judged people wrongly before. Bryce had fooled her completely, she thought wryly.

"I was under the notion that the Chamber of Riches was just a legacy," Jake spoke up for the first time. "Is there actually such a thing? I thought it just amounted to a few crown jewels that were on display in some of your country's museums.''

Once again Marcus studied the American Stanbury with slow deliberation and Dominique wondered what was going on behind his dark, handsome features.

Like her, he'd already suspected that King Michael's disappearance had been more than just an accident. Was he thinking that someone in this room, someone close to the family was responsible for such a hideous crime? she wondered. The idea was incredible.

Marcus explained, "The people of Edenbourg are aware that a chamber of riches exists and that the hidden wealth backs up this country's monetary strength. Other than King Michael or acting King Nicholas, no one knows where this chamber of riches is located. And even if someone learned of its location, the discovery would be profitless. Only the king and his son have a key to its entryway. Unless, of course, this outside someone has the idea he could force his way into the chamber without being caught.''

"Exactly,'' Nicholas added. "And as of right now, anything anyone might say about this murder and Father's disappearance is pure speculation. The only thing we can do is wait for further evidence to be uncovered by the investigators.''

Once again ripples of conversation rose up around the room. However, this time Josephine was content to let the talk continue. Apparently the queen had heard all she wanted to hear. As for Dominique, she'd listened to more than enough. Especially the offensive notion that Nicholas would do something so vile.

"I'm going back to my suite,'' Dominique said in a low voice to Marcus.

He slipped off the arm of the chair and helped her to her feet. "I'll walk with you," he told her. "Do you need to say anything to Prudence?"

Dominique shook her head. Once her lady-in-waiting saw her leaving the room with Marcus, she would purposely avoid following her princess.

Several pairs of eyes observed their exit from the sitting room. Dominique ignored the curious stares. Being linked to Marcus was nothing compared to all the speculations the autopsy report was going to stir up.

Once they were outside in the corridor, Dominique felt herself wilting with the aftermath of the news. Sensing her distress, Marcus curved his arm around the back of her waist and kept it there as they walked.

"Were you surprised by the findings?" Dominique asked him.

"A part of me was shocked that such a gruesome thing could have happened here in this quiet, friendly country. But as you and I discovered that day at the cliff, all didn't seem to add up."

She shook her head in total dismay. "Yes, I've been clinging to the idea that Father wasn't in the car. I felt in my heart that he wasn't dead. But to hear Nicholas actually say the police think he might have been kidnapped was—it's terrifying, Marcus. Do you think that's what actually happened? Do you think someone is keeping him against his will?"

He glanced behind them before he answered. "It's looking more and more that way. Especially since his body hasn't turned up anywhere."

She shuddered at the thought and he looked down at her with concern. "I'm worried about you, Dominique. This is too much shock and stress for you to be dealing with."

"There's nothing to be done about it, Marcus. Until the police find my father, I'll just have to keep praying that he'll return to us safe and sound. But there's no need for you to worry about me. I'm strong and healthy."

"Did you go see the royal physician?" he wanted to know.

She nodded. Two days ago, she'd visited Dr. Wallcott, who was kept on staff for the royal family and their servants. The older man had been caring for the Stanburys for many years, even before Dominique was born, and she knew it had upset him to learn of her plight. But he'd not admonished her. Instead, he'd urged her to take extra care of herself.

"Physically he says the baby and I are doing fine. But he is concerned about my emotional health. He understands the difficult position I'm in."

"You didn't explain to him, about the father, did you?"

A tiny frown marred her forehead as she glanced up at him. "Why, no. Not about Bryce. If that's what you mean."

"Good. I don't want anyone to doubt I'm the father. Not even Dr. Wallcott."

He was expecting her to marry him, she thought sickly. He'd made up his mind to claim her baby as his own even if it ruined his career. She didn't understand why he would make such a sacrifice for her. Or maybe it wasn't for her, she thought sadly, but for his lost king.

The two of them followed several more twists and turns of the lofty hallway, then stopped outside the door to her suite.

"Would you like to come in for coffee? Or do you need to get back to the sitting room?" she asked.

"Nicholas can do without me for a few minutes," he assured her. "I've already advised him on what and what not to say once he begins speaking with the press. Besides," he added as he followed her into the foyer, "I've been wanting to talk to you privately."

There was that word again, she thought. The last time he'd talked with her *privately*, he'd proposed marriage. She couldn't imagine him saying anything that could surprise her more. Other than the words *I love you*.

But Marcus Kent was not going to be saying those words to her. Or to any woman. The sooner she realized that, the sooner she could get on with her life.

# Chapter Nine

"If you want to take a seat, I'll get the coffee going," she said as the two of them entered her quiet suite.

He nodded. "I'll be out on the balcony," he told her. "After the ordeal in the sitting room, I feel the need of some fresh air."

The coffeemaker was the instant drip kind and in only a matter of a few short minutes, Dominique was carrying a tray with the strong brew and slices of pound cake out to the balcony.

It was still a fine, warm day, but Dominique could see a bank of rain clouds forming in the distance. Soon lightning would be dancing over the ocean and a spring storm would wash the streets of Old Stanbury.

Marcus was standing by the balustrade looking down on the city, but the moment he heard her footstep he turned and hurried over to take the tray from her hands.

"This isn't the way things work, Dominique," he scolded lightly. "Princesses are waited on by others. Not the other way around."

She laughed out loud and the release felt good after the tense moments they had just endured in the family sitting room.

"Oh, Marcus, this isn't the medieval age. And you have to remember I haven't been living as a princess for the past four years. I like doing things for myself and for others. I'm not lazy or helpless."

He placed the tray on the round glass table, then helped her into one of the wrought-iron chairs. As he took a seat across from her, she pushed a mug and a small plate with a slice of cake toward him.

"I never imagined you were either of those things," he said, then looked at her with a new thought. "Now that you're going to have a child, what are you going to do about your plans for the education center you wanted to build?"

She sighed, then after a careful sip of coffee, said, "I hope I can continue with the plan. As I just said, I like helping people. Especially children. But of course, everything will hinge on how my family reacts to my having a baby. If all hell breaks loose I may have to move away and support myself."

The implication of her words caused a deep scowl to hood his golden-brown eyes. "You won't be doing any such thing, Dominique!" he said sharply. "Put that idea from your mind right now!"

Dominique bristled. "I am not your wife yet, Marcus. And if that's the demanding attitude you took with Liza, it's little wonder you're not still a husband!"

His scowl grew into a glower as he took in the thrust of her chin and the spark of defiance in her green eyes. She said things to him that no woman ever had in the past. Which was surprising. Four years ago when she'd left for college in New England, Dominique had been shy. Even uncertain as to when and how she should speak. Apparently, living in the West had changed her in more ways than one, he thought crossly.

"I never used a demanding attitude with my ex-wife and I think it's rather presumptuous of you to accuse me of something you know nothing about," he said with a force that matched the approaching rain clouds.

Undaunted by his fierce response, she studied him with raised eyebrows. "If that's so, then why are you using it with me?"

Her question caught him so totally off guard that all he could do was simply stare at her. And then he almost laughed to think that questions from statesmen and kings and presidents never rattled him. But for a moment this feminine form of fire sitting across from him had made him lose his tongue.

"All right, Dominique," he said more gently. "If I sounded as though I was being bullish, then I apologize. I only want you to understand that I'm not about to let you leave your home. Unless it's to live with me as my wife."

Even though her heart was in turmoil, she had to smile. "And that's not being demanding?"

He heaved out a frustrated breath, then came around the table and pulled out a chair directly next to her. Easing down on the edge of the seat, he leaned toward her, his face only inches from hers.

"Dominique, I'm not trying to be demanding. Just realistic. I want what's best for you. I want to give you and the baby the shelter of my name."

That he wanted to do those things for her amazed Dominique. Yet it wasn't enough. She was in a precarious position; she'd be the first one to admit it. But marriage was something she'd always considered serious and lifelong. To marry a man who didn't love her would be sacrificing her dreams.

"Marcus, when a woman marries she wants more than just her husband's name. She wants passion and—"

"And?"

Love. She'd almost said the word to him, but instead she'd swallowed it down. It was humiliating to know a man had made her pregnant without loving her. Now another man wanted to make her his wife without giving her his love. She couldn't take a double whammy of rejection.

She drew in a deep breath then let it out. "And I understand if we were to marry—we—it would be only for appearances."

He looked at her blankly for a few seconds and then an odd sort of gleam entered his topaz eyes.

"Is that what's bothering you?" he murmured. "Is that why you've been hesitating about giving me an answer?"

Her face hot with embarrassment, she looked away from him and toward the approaching storm. "Feeling wanted by her husband is important to a woman. At least, it would be important to me."

His reply didn't come in words. Instead, he gathered her hands in his and she looked at him with confusion as he gently drew her to her feet.

"If it's passion you're worried about, Dominique, I can supply you with plenty of that."

The quietly spoken words were full of promise and totally unexpected. Surprise parted her lips and tugged her gaze back to his face.

"Are you saying the marriage would be more than platonic?"

As if to convey his message in clearer terms, he bent his head and rubbed his cheek lightly against hers. Instantly, Dominique felt her bones turn to sponge and air lodge in her lungs. The effect he had on her was more than enough to muddle her senses. It was downright frightening.

"We don't necessarily have to have a marriage in name only," he explained. "You're a beautiful woman, Dominique. A man would have to be crazy not to want to share a bed with you."

For a man, sharing a bed with a woman was something entirely different than sharing his heart with her, Dominique silently argued. Bryce had more than proved that adage. As for Marcus, she had yet to hear him voice anything about loving her. And even worse, she didn't expect him to.

In a weak flutter of protest, she flattened her hands against his chest and lightly pushed him away from her. "Marcus, that's not exactly what I meant."

Taking hold of her shoulders, he looked at her. Frustration twisted his features and darkened his brown eyes. "You just told me you wanted passion in your marriage. Now you're saying it's something else. I can't understand you, Dominique, if you don't speak your mind and make it clear to me what it is you want."

She wanted to stomp on his toe for being so blind. He should be able to see and understand it was his love she wanted. Nothing else.

Dominique countered him with a question. "Why did Liza marry you?"

He stared at her as though her mind had suddenly sailed off into space, and then frowned with a bit of self-mockery. "I suppose you'd have to get the exact answer from her," he said. "To this day, I'm not sure why the woman married me. At first I believed it was because she loved me. But later, I can only assume it was for my position as king's high counsel and the social circle that being my wife put her into.''

If that was so, then he'd truly had his heart crushed, Dominique thought sadly. And losing the baby must have been a final, fatal blow. He must have felt as though the world had crashed in on him. But that didn't mean everything had ended. Love would find him again. All he had to do was give his heart a second chance.

''Well, as far as I'm concerned, position or social status has nothing to do with marriage,'' she said firmly. ''It's all about sharing yourself with someone and being a family. It's all about love.''

As soon as the last word was out, his hands dropped away from her as though she'd just confessed to having a deadly, contagious disease.

''Love!'' he said with a groan, frustration twisting his features. ''Oh, Dominique! I understand most young women have romantic fantasies about a fairy-tale marriage and I wish that things could be that way for you. But a charming prince with special powers to create happily-ever-afters just doesn't exist. You and your baby's welfare is the only thing that should be running through your mind. You are a Stanbury,'' he reminded her as if her pregnancy had affected her memory. ''A member of the royal family of Edenbourg. Your child should come into this world under the sanctity of married parents. Not under a black mark that could follow him for the rest of his life.''

The truth of what he was saying caused her to groan with guilt and anguish. Quickly, she turned her back to him rather than confront the censure on his face.

''You are right, Marcus,'' she whispered in a shaky

voice. "My child shouldn't be punished for my reckless behavior. His or her name shouldn't be marred because I was misled by a slick-talking rake. But can't you see? I've already made one mistake with a man who didn't love me."

He didn't make any sort of response and in a flash she twisted back around and tilted her face up to his. Her expression dared him to deny what she was about to say next. "You don't love me either, Marcus. I'd be making my second mistake with you."

Marcus cursed beneath his breath. It was beyond him how she could be thinking about love at a time like this. Love had nothing to do with it. Common sense was the thing that should be ruling her head. And his...

"Dominique, take a good look at me. I'm living proof that love doesn't last. In fact, the more I think about it, the more I doubt that the emotion even exists. It's just a state of mind. A euphoric daze that people slip into for a while and then it fades. The right choices in life can't be built on such a fleeting, nebulous emotion."

"That's because you had your hopes dashed by Liza," she reasoned. "And the divorce has left you cynical. But I'm not about to let Bryce ruin me in the way you've allowed Liza to ruin you. He isn't worth it. I truly believe that someday I'll find a man who loves me just for me."

"And that's more important to you than giving your baby a name? Giving him a father?" he asked with angry disbelief.

Shaking her head with defeat, she turned and walked over to the edge of the balcony. With her hands resting on the wide stone balustrade, she gazed out at the on-coming clouds. In the past few minutes the sky had grown darker and lightning was beginning to dance in jagged streaks amongst the boiling thunderheads. There was no doubt they were headed for a rainstorm. Just as surely as she was bound for a heartache.

"Dominique, you haven't answered me."

She looked up to see he was standing beside her, his face lined with angry impatience. She closed her eyes against him and the approaching storm.

"Marcus, it's clear to both of us that you're offering to marry me out of a sense of duty and honor. To my father and my family. And all of this uproar over King Michael's disappearance has made you even more determined to shield the Stanburys from any more scandal. That's not a good reason to become someone's husband."

His short laugh was caustic. "If more marriages were based on duty and honor there would be far fewer divorces."

Clamping her lips in a tight line, she shook her head. "I'd hate to think my husband was staying with me out of a sense of duty. That's the coldest, most clinical thing I've ever heard!"

Strange, Marcus thought, but there was nothing cold and clinical about the way he felt at this moment. About the fire that singed his veins every time he came within any distance of Dominique.

"In your opinion, Dominique. In mine, it's intelligent and much more reasonable."

A cool wind was beginning to blow in from the rain clouds, but it was Marcus's words that were chilling Dominique to the bone.

"I wish I could make you understand that marrying only for the sake of the baby would be a giant mistake. In the end we would both be miserable and at each other's throats. A child can't grow and flourish under those conditions.'' She swallowed at the tightness in her throat, then glanced up at him beseechingly. ''I want more for my child than that. I want more for me. If that makes me selfish, then so be it.''

Folding his arms against his chest, he too stared out at the fast-approaching storm. ''Maybe the problem you have about marrying me has nothing to do with love,'' he said flatly.

Her gaze whipped back to his face. ''It has everything to do with it!'' she countered hotly.

He glared back at her. ''No. Any woman with an ounce of common sense wouldn't be worrying about love at a time like this. And the more I think about it, the more I'm convinced that your real concern is over marrying a commoner. Especially one who's already had a disastrous marriage end with his wife divorcing him!''

She gasped with disbelief. How could he accuse her of such a thing? she wondered wildly. She'd always held him in such high regard, and furthermore he knew it! He was being insufferable and for no good reason that she could see.

''That's incredible, Marcus! I thought you knew me! I thought you understood that being a princess of Edenbourg is a very small part of who I am and what is important to me. And it's definitely not a person's name or bloodline!''

His twisted lips jeered at her words. ''The day we went to Chauncey's Inn I told you I wasn't good enough to be your husband and you wanted to argue the point. But now...I think you were only trying to flatter me that day. I can see now that we've come down to the bottom line, you've realized that you'd rather be an unwed mother than lower yourself to marrying me!''

That he could accuse her of such outrageous bigotry filled her with such fury that she had to take several breaths before she could finally push any sort of comment past her lips.

"Please leave, Marcus. And I would very much appreciate you not ever speaking to me again!''

Drops of cold rain began to splatter all around them, but Marcus continued to glare at her with fire in his eyes.

"Gladly, Dominique! I'm tired of trying to help a woman who doesn't want or need my support. You think you have all the right beliefs and answers, so from this point on you can deal with the problem yourself!''

He stalked off the balcony and back through the door that entered her sitting room. Oblivious to the increasing rain, Dominique remained where she was as she tried to collect her heated senses.

What had she done? she wondered. Had she ruined the best thing that could have ever happened to her? Or saved her heart from an even bigger ache than the one it was feeling now?

Two days later, Marcus was in his office trying to concentrate on a proposed national military budget, when his secretary announced that King Nicholas was on his way to see him.

It was just as well that his work was going to be interrupted, he thought. He was getting very little accomplished and he had Dominique to thank for that. Since their argument on the balcony his thoughts had been even more consumed with her.

He felt wretched about some of the things he'd said

to her. But he couldn't go to her and take them back. For one thing, she'd made it plain she wanted the connection between them broken. For another, it would be misleading to try to snatch back his words, when deep down he felt he was right. Love had no place in his life. It was a costly investment, full of risk and pain. Her experience back in the States ought to have already proven that to Dominique, he thought crossly.

A light knock sounded on the door just as Marcus was placing the important file to one side of his desk. He looked up to see King Nicholas entering the office. The other man's expression was grim and Marcus could only surmise that things weren't going any better for the acting king than they were for his counsel.

"I'm sorry to be interrupting you like this, Marcus," he said as he made himself comfortable in a wingback chair positioned in front of Marcus's desk. "And you're probably thinking it would have been simpler to have picked up the phone and called you, but frankly I've had all of the telephone I want this morning."

Since the news of Herbert's murder had hit the press two days ago, the castle had been bombarded with calls from the public. Marcus was aware that many of them had been nastily directed at Nicholas. Some of them accusing him outright of killing his own father to acquire the throne.

From the look on the king's face this morning, the awful weight of suspicion was wearing him down.

"Are the calls still coming in?" Marcus asked.

"They're down to several an hour now rather than several a minute," he said in a harried voice. "But most of them are still directed at me."

"You can't let it get to you, Your Highness. The public is a fickle thing. Once the truth of this whole matter comes out, they'll be worshiping you for taking up your father's reins."

Nicholas swiped a weary hand over his face. "Yes. But when might that be? A year from now? Two years from now? How can I continue to do my work or even go about my daily life when people are accusing me of killing my own father? It's ludicrous for anyone to think I could have ever had a harmful thought against the man!"

Marcus got up from his seat behind the desk and went over to a small table holding a coffeemaker and all the fixings. Without asking, he poured a cup for Nicholas and carried it to him.

"Here. You look as if you could use this."

Nicholas gratefully accepted the cup. "Thanks, Marcus. Although I really don't have time for it. I'm to meet with the royal treasurer in a few minutes. He believes the citizens of Edenbourg are eventually going to demand that all government records be audited. To make sure that I, or someone else in the family, hasn't been stealing. Along with murdering," he added angrily.

Marcus shook his head with wonder as he poured himself a cup of coffee, then carried it around to his seat behind the desk. "You know, a year ago, when the Duke of Thortonburg's daughter was kidnapped, I told myself nothing so shocking or evil could ever happen in our own country. The subjects of Edenbourg are all kind people, loyal to their king and their country. I truly believed they would never do harm to either. But now, it saddens me to admit I could be wrong."

"Maybe you're looking in the wrong direction," Nicholas said as he leveled his gaze on Marcus. "And I believe you are. I believe an outsider, not a countryman, is responsible for my father's disappearance."

With a grim nod, Marcus sipped the coffee, then placed the cup and saucer on his desk. "I hope you are right. Not that it will make any difference as to finding King Michael."

"Do you think that's possible, Marcus? That by some miraculous chance the authorities will find my father alive?"

Marcus shrugged. "The hope of that looks dim to me. But I refuse to rule out the possibility."

Nicholas sighed. "Rebecca is devastated over this whole thing. It's breaking her heart to have her husband called a murderer. And being from the States, she still doesn't understand the workings of a monarchy or why the throne is so important. I think sometimes she wishes I wasn't the one to inherit the position of king."

"She was aware of your future destination before she married you," Marcus reasoned.

Nicholas smiled wanly. "That's true. But she wasn't expecting me to step into my father's shoes so quickly or under such grisly circumstances."

It was no secret that Nicholas and Rebecca had married for love. Not because King Michael had ordered his son to take a bride. Their feelings for each other were often evident in the smiles and touches they exchanged. Marcus had to admit he'd watched the couple with a bit of envy. He'd wanted that same sort of closeness, of sharing and caring with Liza. But when she'd walked away without a backward glance, it had convinced him that love was for other people, like Nicholas and Rebecca. It wasn't meant for him.

"Rebecca is a strong, devoted wife. She'll make it through this with you, Your Highness. You're lucky in that regard."

In spite of his worries, Nicholas was able to smile.

"Yes, I am lucky," he echoed Marcus's sentiments. "And I'm not going to give up hope that Father will be found alive."

"Have you rescheduled LeAnn's christening yet? Or does Rebecca want to wait until things quiet down?"

Nicholas sighed. "Actually we haven't had time to discuss our daughter's christening with all this public chaos going on. I'll discuss it with her tonight and let you know."

Marcus picked up his coffee cup. "Was there something else in particular you wanted to speak to me about?"

Nicholas groaned, then quickly glancing at his watch, he rose to his feet. "Actually, I was going to talk to you about Dominique. But I've got to be going."

At the mention of Dominique's name, everything inside Marcus went still. "What about Dominique?" he asked as casually as he could.

Nicholas crossed the room and deposited his empty cup on the table with the coffeemaker. "When we discussed her last week, you told me you believed she was pulling out of her doldrums and coming to terms with all that had happened. And I agreed. She appeared to be doing better. But I saw her for a few minutes this morning and, if anything, she seemed worse than ever before. I'm worried that she's ill."

Marcus studied the brown liquid in his cup as images of Dominique floated to the forefront of his mind. She was too much of a romantic. Too softhearted for her own good, he thought dismally. She wanted love for herself and her baby. The devotion and support he'd offered her had meant little or nothing.

Carefully choosing his words, Marcus said, "Hearing that Herbert was murdered set her back, I think."

With his hand on the doorknob, Nicholas paused and glanced back at Marcus with a puzzled frown. "I understand she liked the old man. We all did. But the explanation of the driver's death backs up Dominique's theory that Father might still be alive. You would think the news would have made her happy, even hopeful. Instead, she looks as though she's lost her best friend. Have you spoken with her?"

Still not meeting the other man's gaze, Marcus said, "Not since the results of the autopsy were announced."

"Then I'd appreciate it if you'd give her another visit," Nicholas told him. "The whole family needs to be strong right now."

Dominique certainly needed someone to give her strength, Marcus thought. But it wasn't him. She wanted something he couldn't give.

"Isabel should be the one visiting your sister. Not me," Marcus brusquely argued. "I have no influence with Dominique."

Nicholas shot him a pointed smile, then as he stepped from the office, he called over his shoulder. "I happen to think you do."

Once the door closed behind his new king, Marcus banged his fist against the top of the desk. What was the man thinking, that he and Dominique were close?

With a whispered curse, he closed his eyes and pinched the bridge of his nose.

From where Marcus was sitting, the two of them would never be close again. And the whole notion was tearing him apart.

# *Chapter Ten*

Later that afternoon Dominique was lying on her bed, staring up at the heavy velvet canopy draped over the four elaborately carved posts. It was a royal bed. The wood was hand-crafted and put together hundreds of years ago by skilled carpenters. Generations of her family had slept in the bed before her. And it was commonly assumed that later her children would be given the same due. Just as Nicholas's and Isabel's children would be privileged to live in the castle with all its ornate trappings.

Her hand crept to the bulge of baby growing at the low point of her belly. Would the child she was carrying be truly accepted here? she wondered. Would he or she eventually be recognized as a member of the royal family, or shunned because there was no father?

Telling Marcus she couldn't marry him should have given her some sort of relief from all this mental anguish. But it hadn't. If anything, she'd been more miserable these past two days than she'd ever been in her life.

Dominique wanted to give her child everything it needed and deserved. Including a good father. Which she knew Marcus would be. The nurturing and guidance he would bestow upon a child would lay the foundation for a strong, responsible adult. Just the sort of person her father would expect his grandchild to grow to be.

But Marcus didn't love her. And in all good conscience, she couldn't bind him to a situation that would make him miserable. Right now he believed love wasn't important. But later he would see that a marriage without that main ingredient would be an empty union. Eventually, he might even want his freedom so that he could search for someone he could love.

*If more marriages were based on duty and honor there would be far fewer divorces.*

The memory of Marcus's words goaded her until she raised up on the side of the bed and dropped her head into her hands.

Maybe he was right, she thought wretchedly. Maybe it hadn't mattered to her mother long ago when Josephine's parents had ordered her to marry a man she'd never met. At least the marriage had lasted.

The thought of her mother had her quickly sliding off the bed and pushing her bare feet into her shoes. If anyone could advise her about arranged marriages, it would be the queen. But whether the woman would want to talk about such an intimate thing with Dominique would be anyone's guess. The only thing she could do was try. For her baby's sake and her own.

Prudence was out running an errand, so she didn't have to give her lady-in-waiting an excuse for leaving the suite. Which was a good thing. Prudence was beginning to suspect that something out of the ordinary had occurred between Dominique and Marcus. Her lady-in-waiting had even gone so far as to question Dominique about their leaving the sitting room together two days ago. But Dominique couldn't bring herself to tell Prudence that everything between Marcus and herself, including their friendship, had ended.

The corridor leading to Josephine's suite was quiet, and Dominique met no one on her way. Two royal guards stood at the door. The sight of the two uniformed men brought home the unnerving fact that someone evil was lurking in their midst.

She struggled to push the dark thought away as she entered her mother's suite and found her sitting on the couch, staring quietly off into space.

For a moment, the sight chilled Dominique. It wasn't like Josephine to sit idly, and she never allowed her mind to be preoccupied with anything other than the task she was performing at the moment. For as long as Dominique could remember, Josephine had always thrown herself headlong into charity functions and social causes. But now, with King Michael's disappearance, Nicholas and Marcus both feared for the queen's safety and were reluctant to give her the freedom to leave the palace grounds.

"Mother? May I visit with you for a few minutes?"

Josephine's smooth profile jerked toward the entrance of the room with a start, then just as instantly a smile lit her face as she spotted Dominique.

"Of course, my daughter. Please, come in."

She patted the empty spot beside her on the rich brocade couch. Dominique obeyed while feeling as if she were ten again, rather than twenty-one and pregnant.

"We haven't spoken since we received the news

about Herbert,'' the queen said as she flicked a spot of imaginary dust from her navy blue skirt. ''I'm curious to know what you've been thinking, my dear.''

In all truth, Dominique had hardly been able to think about the issue of her missing father. Her mind had been consumed with Marcus and the awful way they had parted.

''I'm so sorry Herbert's life was taken in such a ghastly way,'' she said to her mother. ''It's difficult to believe that anyone could harm such a kindly old gentleman.''

Josephine inclined her head in agreement. ''It's apparent that he lost his life because he was with King Michael. Otherwise, there would be no advantage or reason to take his life.''

Dominique smoothed her hands together, then glanced around the ornate living room. The furnishings were the same as they had been years before. Rich silks and velvets draped the windows, deep wool covered the floor. It was a quiet, austere room. Hardly the sort of atmosphere that invited an intimate chat. But Dominique wouldn't let herself be put off. She needed her mother now. Probably more than she'd ever needed her.

''Mother,'' she began carefully, ''what do you think about our American relatives?''

Josephine's eyebrows lifted ever so slightly at her question. ''I believe your father would be very pleased that his brother has finally come back to make amends with him. Frankly, I'm glad Edward and his sons decided to remain on the palace grounds. Having them here is a diversion from all this horrible occurrence connected to your father. And Sammy is a delight. It's been a very long time since a toddler has been inside these old castle walls." She paused, then studied her daughter with new regard. "Why do you ask?"

Apparently Josephine held no suspicious thoughts toward Edward Stanbury or Jake and Luke. Otherwise, she would have already voiced them. As for her pleasure over Sammy, it was comforting to know her mother had a soft spot for all children.

Deciding it would be best not to mention any suspicions she held toward the American Stanburys, Dominique answered blithely. "No reason in particular. I just wondered how you'd been getting along with them, that's all."

Josephine reassured her with a small smile. "Splendidly. And what about you?"

Dominique forced a smile on her face. "Oh, well, Isabel and Pru think I haven't been getting along with anyone here lately," she attempted to joke. "I suppose I need to work on being more sociable with everyone."

To Dominique's surprise, her mother reached over and gently patted her knee.

"I know how close you always were to your father, Dominique. I understand this can't be an easy time for you."

King Michael's disappearance had been devastating to her, Dominique silently agreed. But it was only a small reason for the turmoil in her heart and the whole misconception by her family burdened her with deep guilt.

"I miss Father terribly," she said in a strained voice. "The castle isn't the same without him."

A small sigh escaped Josephine and then she said in a low voice, "No. I didn't realize how quiet this place would be until he was gone."

Dominique's sidelong glance at her mother was

thoughtful. "Mother," she began cautiously, "I've never talked to you about this before—and I hope you won't think I'm intruding, but—"

Curious now, Josephine turned on the cushion to face her daughter more squarely. "But what, my dear? What are you trying to ask me?"

Dominique drew in a deep breath and wondered why she found it so hard to communicate with her mother. It had always been so easy to talk to her father. He was brusque, but always open and ready to speak his mind. With Josephine's quiet, reserved manner, no one, not even her children, ever really knew what was in her thoughts.

"I've often wondered—what did you think all those years ago when you were told it had been arranged for you to marry Father?"

Surprise flickered in Josephine's eyes and for a moment Dominique decided she was going to gently change the subject. But then her mother's expression softened and her eyes changed to a dreaminess that Dominique had never seen before.

"To be honest, Dominique, I was outraged and defiant. I didn't want to marry a man I'd never met. Especially one from another country. But as Princess of Wynborough it was my duty to obey my parents' wishes and do my part to solidify the country's union with Edenbourg. So I had little choice in the matter. I kept my true feelings to myself and went forward with as much dignity as I could."

*I kept my true feelings to myself.* Those words were like a book opening up inside Dominique and for the first time in her young life, she could read and understand her mother.

Early on, Josephine had been groomed and prepared

to take her place amongst noble blood. Whether it be the Wynboroughs' or the Stanburys'. Fifty years ago, a woman, especially from a royal family, had no choice in the direction her life took. Honor, duty, dignity. Those things came first and personal feelings last. Marcus held those same beliefs and Dominique knew it shocked and angered him because she could not be like her mother. But Dominique wanted love and happiness in her life and she wasn't sure Josephine had ever had either.

"When did you finally meet Father?"

A wry smile touched the queen's lips. "On the day of my wedding."

Amazed, Dominique studied the regal beauty of her mother's face. "Oh. I can't imagine how difficult that must have been," she murmured as much to herself as to Josephine. "To place your hand in a stranger's and all the while knowing he was going to be your husband for the rest of your life."

"It wasn't easy," Josephine agreed. "At that time your father was very handsome, but equally fierce-looking. I felt as though I were being handed over to a Viking warrior. I trembled throughout the ceremony and for days afterward."

New respect and admiration for her mother filled Dominique as she thought about all the trials the other woman had endured back then. Josephine had been forced to leave the security of her home and family in Wynborough and travel to a far-off country and make a new life with a stranger. Dominique wasn't at all sure she could have been that brave.

"Was it difficult to adjust to being his wife?" Dominique wanted to know.

Josephine smiled and Dominique was instantly bemused by the tiny glow of light in her mother's eyes.

"At first," she admitted. "I was timid and your father impatient. But then I began to learn Michael's habits and personality and he began to learn mine and it wasn't so hard. Especially when we both agreed on having several children."

The mention of children brought home the very reason Dominique was troubled and for a moment she considered telling her mother she was with child. But the thought of Marcus and her baby's reputation held her back.

"Then your marriage turned out to be better than you expected?"

Josephine looked at her daughter as though she found it comical that Dominique had to ask such a thing.

"Of course it turned out better. Back in Wynborough, when my parents told me of my future fate, I had to fight the urge to run away, to do anything that would spare me from marrying a stranger. I was convinced my life would be ruined forever. You see, Dominique, as a young woman all I'd ever dreamed about or wanted was to marry a man I loved. I believed my parents were taking that dream away from me."

And how that must have hurt, Dominique thought. How disillusioned Josephine must have felt when she'd traveled to Edenbourg to become the wife of a man she'd never met.

She looked at her mother, wondering how she could ask her if she had ever found true love with Michael Stanbury. But the problem of posing the question was instantly taken out of her hands as Josephine began to speak softly once again.

"Instead, they had given me a dream come true. At the time, I just didn't have the wisdom to see it."

Dominique's eyebrows lifted. "Then you...grew to love Father?"

A tender smile lifted the queen's lips. "I tried to resist his charms, but in the end it was impossible. I fell in love with him almost instantly. I loved his fierceness, his laugh, his touch. He became a part of me and I a part of him." Her eyes welled with unexpected tears as she looked at Dominique. "I never thought I would lose him this way. I never thought I could miss anyone so much."

Torn by the sight of her mother's misery, Dominique instantly reached for her hands and held on to them tightly. "Oh, Mother, I'm so sorry. But I believe we will get him back. Somehow. Some way."

"I pray that we will, Dominique," she whispered earnestly. "I pray that I will be given a second chance to tell your father how much I love him. How much I've always loved him."

Dominique tried to swallow down the tears burning her throat. "I'm sure wherever father is, he knows how you feel about him."

Josephine shook her head with regret. "It's never been easy for me to express my feelings toward others. Even toward your father. I never told him in exact words that I loved him. I simply took it for granted that he knew how I felt about him." She sighed deeply, then turned a pointed look on Dominique. "That's my one regret, daughter. So I'm sharing this difficult lesson with you today. If you do fall in love with a man, don't hold the truth of your feelings back from him. Tell him how you feel before it's too late."

*Tell him how you feel.* Everything inside Dominique

suddenly went still. Would it make a difference, she wondered, if she told Marcus she loved him? Probably not. He didn't believe in the emotion. He didn't want it. But at least she wouldn't be burdened with the regret of not trying.

Squeezing her mother's hands, she said, "Thank you for sharing this with me, Mother. It's helped me more than you know."

Josephine smiled with tender affection. "I'm glad. Now tell me, dear daughter, what is this all about? Have you found a young man you want to marry?"

A spurt of crazy hope dashed through Dominique, but she quickly squashed it down. She'd told Marcus she never wanted to speak with him again and he was a man of great pride. Even if she initiated an invitation for them to meet, he might refuse to see her.

"Maybe. I'm not sure yet."

Quickly, she rose to her feet, then bent and kissed her mother's cheek. "Right now I hope you'll forgive me for leaving so abruptly, but there's something I need to attend to."

Josephine waved her away and Dominique dashed out of the suite and hurried back to her own. Prudence had returned from her errand and stepped through the swinging doors of the kitchenette the moment she heard her princess's footsteps.

"My goodness, what's all the rush about?" Prudence asked as she watched Dominique sink down on the couch and struggle to catch her breath. "Has something happened?"

Yes, Dominique thought. She'd just learned that she was more like her mother than she'd ever dreamed. She'd been hiding her true feelings, her real self, for a long time. But unlike Josephine, she wasn't going to wait until it was too late to do something about it.

"Not yet," Dominique answered, then bounded from the couch and crossed the room to a small writing desk.

As she scratched out a quick note on pale pink stationery, Prudence slowly approached her.

"What do you mean? Are you expecting some sort of news to break about your father?"

She folded the note and slipped it into an envelope. After sealing it, she handed the message to her lady-in-waiting. "This has nothing to do with my father's disappearance," she answered. "I want you to deliver this personally to Marcus. I'm not sure if he'll be in his office or apartment. Just find him and do it quickly."

Prudence looked as if she was going to question Dominique further. But something must have changed the other young woman's mind because she quickly turned on her heel and headed toward the foyer.

"I won't return until I find him," she tossed the promise over her shoulder.

Since Marcus had stepped into the position of king's high counsel, he'd never doubted a decision he'd made concerning the country, the king or even his own ill-fated marriage to Liza. He'd always been certain that he'd chosen the best path for everyone involved.

Until he'd made the choice to walk away from Dominique.

The thought made him rake both hands through his hair with helpless frustration. He shouldn't be feeling this miserable or torn, he told himself as he prowled restlessly from room to room in his small apartment. He should be relieved that Dominique had refused his proposal.

After Liza, he'd sworn never to marry again. He hadn't wanted a second chance to have a wife or child. The pain of losing them both had been more than enough to convince Marcus that love or marriage was not his cup of tea.

But if he was going to be honest with himself, he had to admit he'd never wanted anything as much as he wanted for Dominique to become his wife.

It didn't make sense, he mentally argued. Why did he feel this desperate need to marry her?

The question caused him to pause long enough to sink into a stuffed armchair and stare out the picture window overlooking the palace grounds.

His job demanded devotion to his king, and Marcus had always given it loyally. But his position as king's high counsel did not include marrying the king's pregnant daughter to save face for the Stanbury family. It didn't mean it was his responsibility to give the baby a father or secure its future. Yet he wanted to do all those things. He wanted the child to be his. He wanted Dominique to be his.

Why? he asked himself for what seemed like the hundredth time. Isabel was King Michael's daughter also, but if she was unwed and pregnant he wouldn't feel inclined to marry her. Because he didn't love her, he reasoned. He loved Dominique.

The last thought jolted him like the strike of a fist against his chin. For long moments he stared blindly out the window as emotions too big to contain began to roil inside him.

Dear Lord, what was he going to do now? he prayed. How was he going to convince Dominique that he wanted to do more than protect her? How was he going to make her see that he wanted to have a shared life with her, have children together, grow old together? He'd told her more than once that he no longer believed in love. He'd specified in clear terms to her that he didn't want or need that sort of devotion from her or any woman. She would probably take great pleasure in throwing those very words back in his face.

But he had to try, he decided. He had to make her see that the three of them could be happy together if she would only give him the chance to prove it.

With a rush of hopeful excitement, he jumped to his feet, then glanced at the telephone.

He could call to make sure Dominique was in her suite. But he didn't want to take the chance that she might refuse to see him. Better to have the element of surprise on his side, he thought as he hurried out the door.

The storm of two days ago had cleared away and the late-afternoon sun was warm and pleasant on his back as he made his way toward the castle. For the first time in days, he noticed spring had truly arrived and flowers were beginning to bloom along the walkways and the carefully tended beds scattered across the sloping lawns of the palace grounds.

Seeing the colorful blossoms made Marcus wonder if the roses had also begun to bud. He knew the precious flower was one of Dominique's favorites. If he could snatch one before he made his way up to her suite, it couldn't hurt his cause to offer her the symbol of love.

The notion had him changing directions at the last minute and cutting through the garden in the back court-yard of the castle. Here the sun felt even warmer and birds whistled and chirped among the tree limbs. After a quick glance at the nearest bushes, he spied a yellow rosebud on the verge of opening its petals. Marcus snapped it off before one of the gardeners spotted him and yelled a loud protest.

He was so intent on getting inside the castle and up to Dominique's suite with the rose that he almost didn't notice the woman sitting at the far end of the garden on a wrought-iron bench. But a flash of movement caught the corner of his vision and he paused on the flagstone to glance in her direction.

Immediately, she rose from the bench and Marcus's heart skipped several beats as he realized it was Dominique standing only a few feet away from him. She was dressed in slim white slacks and a navy blue sweater trimmed in white. Her hair was tied back at the base of her neck with a red silk scarf. The fact that she looked beautiful was no surprise. But the smile on her face caught him totally off guard.

Slowly, he walked toward her as his mind spun with all that he wanted to say. He didn't know where to start. And then suddenly he realized it wasn't words he wanted to give her. He wanted to gather her into his arms. He wanted to worship her face with his hands and lips. He wanted to press her close against him and feel the soft, sweet warmth of her. The intensity of his feelings surprised him even more than finding her in the garden.

Her smile was tentative but warm, and the sight encouraged Marcus, especially after the angry note on which they'd parted.

"Thank you for coming to meet with me, Marcus," she said quickly. "I'm sure you're wondering why I—"

He suddenly frowned. "Coming to meet you?" he repeated blankly. "How did you know I was on my way to see you?"

It was Dominique's turn to look puzzled. "Why, the note, of course. Didn't Pru give it to you?"

He shook his head. "I haven't seen Prudence."

Her expression turned cautious. "Oh. She must have missed you somewhere between your apartment and the castle. I thought—I wrote you a note telling you that I needed to see you. That isn't why you're here?"

"No. I—" He thrust the rose toward her while his heart thumped like a foolish teenager on his first date. "Actually, I was on my way up to your suite."

She accepted the rose, though her expression remained guarded as she continued to study his face. "Really?"

He swallowed and realized with a start that he was nervous. Something that Marcus Kent had never been before. "Yes. I've decided I had to see you. I realized I had to persuade you to marry me, even if it meant begging."

He might as well have knocked her backward with his hand, Dominique thought. The blow wouldn't have been any more shocking.

Clutching the stem of the rose, she stared doubtfully at him. "Why would you want to do that, Marcus? You said—"

He ventured closer and his heart sang with hope when she didn't step back. "Forget everything I've said up until now, Dominique. I was wrong. Wrong about myself and my reasons for wanting to marry you."

Confusion wrinkled her lovely features. "Marcus, please! If you try to tell me that your sense of duty to King Michael isn't what prompted you to propose, I'll know you're lying. It was."

His expression grave, Marcus nodded. "Yes. At first it was duty and a sense of obligation toward my lost king. But things have changed since then. I've changed.''

Dominique's delicate eyebrows arched with wry skepticism. "I find that very difficult to believe, Marcus. You're too set in your ways and beliefs. Duty to your king and country has always come first with you. I can't see that ever changing."

He took another step closer while the urge to reach out and touch her clawed at him like a wild animal desperate to make an escape. "You make me sound old. Is that how you see me? Too old to be capable of changing?"

She made a scoffing noise. "You're a young, virile man, Marcus. But as for you being able to change—I just don't know."

He couldn't bear living unless he had her as his wife. That was how much she had changed him. This love he felt for her had made him a different man.

"Dominique, I want to be your husband. I want to be the father of your baby, the father of all the children we'll hopefully have in the future. Not because I'm duty bound to King Michael or to save you and the baby from scandal."

He reached for her free hand. Bemused, she gave it to him and he immediately tightened his fingers around hers.

"I love you, Dominique. I don't know why I haven't figured that out before. I guess I was too busy trying to fight it," he said regretfully. "I was so determined not to let myself be hurt again, that I refused to believe my heart could have latched on to you in such a deep and needy way."

Dominique stared at him, too scared to let herself

hope, too doubtful to allow any sort of joy to beam through to her heart.

"Two days ago you accused me of not wanting to marry you because you were a divorced commoner," she felt the need to remind him.

He groaned with open shame. "I was angry that day, Dominique. You were turning me down and it hurt. I wanted to lash out at you. I was trying to convince myself and you that love needn't be in our lives. It frustrated me that you were refusing to marry without it."

Gently, his hands curled over her shoulders and his head bent to rub his cheek against hers. "Forgive me, Dominique," he whispered with all the desire burning inside him. "Forgive my stupidity and say you'll marry me."

Still not quite convinced, she said, "For all you know I don't love you, Marcus. Would that matter? Would you still want me as your wife?"

He reared his head back and searched her green eyes. "Yes! Because I have enough love for the both of us. I know I can make you happy. And I'll be a good father to our sons and daughters."

The tender devotion Dominique saw in his eyes was something she'd never seen before and she suddenly knew he was speaking truly from his heart.

With a cry of happiness, she raised on tiptoe and flung her arms around his neck. "Oh, Marcus, my love. My dear sweet love. I sent that note to you asking you to come to the garden to meet me. My intentions were to tell you how much I love you. I'd thought—hoped— that if I explained how I felt about you, you might have a different outlook on our marriage. But now, I feel like you've just handed me a slice of heaven!"

His arms circled her and his head dipped close to hers. "Heaven is having you in my arms, Dominique," he whispered against her lips. "And I never intend to let you go. I won't ever let you walk away from me like Liza did."

She shook her head and tightened her hold on him. "I would never walk away from you, Marcus. I think I knew four years ago that you were the man I was supposed to spend the rest of my life with and I went away to college wondering how or if I could ever make that happen. But then you married and I thought there was no hope. I let myself get involved with Bryce, thinking he would make me forget all about you. But the moment I came back and saw you that morning at Edenbourg Abbey, I realized my feelings for you had never died."

Marcus responded by covering her lips with a kiss that lasted until both of them were gasping for air.

"I don't understand how I could be this lucky," he murmured against the tender curve of her throat. "You and a baby."

Dominique smiled with longing as his hand settled over the small mound of her belly. "I'm the lucky one," she insisted.

"Well, I'm going to be proud to call this little one mine," he promised. "And he or she will get all my love, just the same as our future children."

Tears of joy glazed her green eyes. "I can see why my father wanted you by his side. You're a generous, wonderful man." She sniffed, then looked up at him as a new concern passed through her mind. "Marcus, I will never forgive myself if any of this ruins your reputation. When people hear that I'm already carrying your child—"

Smiling down at her, he shook his head. "You're a

beautiful woman, Dominique. No one will condemn me for getting you with child. Everybody will think it was impossible for me to keep my hands off you. And it very nearly has been,'' he added in a low, sensuous voice.

The smile she returned to him was as intimate as it was promising. "I take that to mean you don't want a long engagement."

He chuckled and as he looked down at the face of the woman who would soon be his wife, he felt as if the garden around them was blazing with bright new color and the whole world was a fresh and wonderful place.

"We don't have time for a long engagement, my darling. We have a baby on the way and the sooner we tell your family, the better."

Dominique's eyes widened. "Now?"

With his hand draped around the back of her waist, he turned her toward the castle. "I can't think of a better time to start our new life together. Can you?"

A new baby. A new life. A love that would last for a lifetime. Yes, Dominique thought gloriously, she could face her family now. She could face anything.

"Right now is perfect," she agreed.

Inside the castle, Dominique and Marcus decided to go to Josephine's suite and give the queen their news before anyone else. But on the way they met Edward and Luke headed for the family sitting room.

"Nicholas has been looking for both of you," Edward said. "I think he has some sort of news about the investigation."

Dominique and Marcus exchanged surprised glances.

"Do you know if Mother is in her suite?" she asked her uncle.

"Everyone is to meet in the family room," Edward explained. "Josephine is probably there already."

"Looks to me like we ought to be calling it the briefing room," Luke spoke up jokingly.

Edward turned a disapproving frown on his son. Luke immediately cleared his throat and cast an apologetic glance at Dominique and Marcus.

"Sorry," he said. "The castle has been full of tension this past week, I was only trying to ease it a little."

Nodding, Marcus graciously accepted Luke Stanbury's apology, then slipped his arm around Dominique's shoulders.

"Actually, we have some news of our own we want to announce," he said as he directed a tender smile down at Dominique. "Shall we go in?"

Dominique was more than ready. She'd loved Marcus for a long time. She was more than ready to shout it to her family and the world.

"Yes," she answered. "I want to speak with Mother before, well, before any bad news Nicholas might have to say."

Inside the sitting room, they found the whole family had already gathered and were sitting in various chairs and on couches and settees around the large room.

Queen Josephine had taken her usual place in her favorite wingback chair facing the fireplace. The moment she saw Dominique and Marcus approaching her, a knowing, satisfied smile settled over her face.

"So this is the man you're going to marry," she said to her daughter.

Marcus cast a puzzled look at Dominique. "How did she know?"

Dominique blushed while Josephine laughed slyly.

"Mothers just know these things," the queen told him.

At that moment Dominique felt a close, binding connection to her mother, one that she knew could never be broken. And the realization only added to her happiness.

"What do you think about my choice of husband?" she asked Josephine.

The queen's pleased smile encompassed her daughter and her soon-to-be son-in-law.

"I couldn't have handpicked a better one for you," she said with conviction.

Immediately, Josephine rose to her feet and clapped her hands to draw the attention of everyone else in the room. When she was certain the whole group was listening, she said, "I have a wonderful announcement to make. Marcus and Dominique have just told me they are to be married."

Hands began to applaud with approval and cries of surprise and joy spread from one end of the room to the other. Isabel and Prudence were the first to rush to her side, and Dominique laughed with joy as they kissed and hugged and congratulated her. Nicholas quickly followed behind them. First kissing his sister, then shaking Marcus's hand.

"You must be a fast worker," Nicholas said to him. "Dominique has only been home for a month!"

Marcus cast Dominique a sly glance. "Well, actually, we got together when she was here for Christmas. We…just didn't say anything to anyone."

"So when is the wedding to be?" Isabel asked with

barely contained excitement. "I hope the engagement is going to be long enough to give us plenty of time to plan a lavish wedding."

Once again Dominique couldn't stop a deep blush from spreading over her face and she looked helplessly up at Marcus.

"I'm afraid the wedding plans will have to be made rather quickly," he answered Isabel. "You see, there's another announcement we have to make."

By now, everyone in the room had gathered around them and as Dominique looked at their faces, she felt no shame or regret. Only joy and pride. Marcus loved her. He was the father of her baby. For now and always.

"Marcus and I are expecting a baby," Dominique said with a happy rush. "In September."

Like the aftermath of a roaring tornado, the room went instantly quiet. All eyes turned to Queen Josephine. Including Dominique's, as she waited anxiously for her mother's response.

"A baby," Josephine repeated with awesome wonder.

"Yes, Mother. Are you displeased?"

The queen stepped forward and took hold of Dominique's hands. "My dear daughter, I couldn't be happier." She leaned forward and kissed both her cheeks, then smiled through happy tears. "You and Marcus bound together with a child. It's exactly the way I always knew it should be. The both of you are going to be very happy."

From the corner of her eye, Dominique could see Marcus glancing down at her. She looked up at him and his eyes were asking her how Josephine had known the two of them belonged together when he'd only just realized it himself.

She smiled at him, while mentally reminding herself to explain to him later about a woman's intuition. To her mother, she whispered joyously, "Thank you, Mother. I only wish Father was here, too. To share this time with Marcus and I. With all of us."

The mention of King Michael had Josephine glancing toward her son, who was still beaming with happy disbelief at his younger sister.

"Nicholas, perhaps it's time we heard your news," Josephine suggested.

Nicholas glanced at his sister Isabel. "Actually," he began, "I believe Isabel is the one with the news. So I'll let her make the announcement."

The whole family, along with Prudence and Rowena, turned their attention to the older of the two Stanbury daughters.

Isabel smiled fondly at her sister. "My news can't begin to measure up to Dominique's wonderful surprise, but it is something I am pleased about." She focused on her mother, then glanced at the anxious faces around her. "In the past hour I've been in contact with Adam Sinclair, my former commanding officer in the Royal Navy. Since he's highly skilled in military intelligence, I've asked him to come to Edenbourg and the Stanbury castle to help us with the ongoing investigation of Father's disappearance. I'm happy to say he's agreed and I'm very hopeful he can help us get King Michael back home with us."

"This is good news," Marcus exclaimed. "I hope his arrival will be soon."

"I agree," Josephine spoke up with a pleased smile. "And I think while we are all gathered here together in the sitting room, we should have a toast for Marcus and

Dominique and also for the coming help of Adam Sinclair.''

''Hear! Hear!'' Nicholas seconded his mother's suggestion.

''Shall I tell Gertie to plan a special dinner for tonight, Your Highness?'' Prudence asked the queen.

Josephine looked around at her family. There was one missing. But soon there would be a new addition. In her heart, she knew Michael would agree that a Stanbury baby was cause for great celebration.

''Yes, Prudence,'' the queen answered. ''Please inform Gertie to prepare a feast for tonight.''

Spirits lifted and happy anticipation suddenly buzzed around the room. Amidst the excitement, Marcus bent his head and whispered in Dominique's ear, ''I just now realized I'm going to have the queen as my mother-in-law.''

Dominique's green eyes twinkled mischievously up at him. ''Want to back out?''

He answered with a chuckle. Then bending his head, he kissed her, letting his lips tell her he would always want to be her husband, always love her. As Josephine had said, the two of them were exactly as they should be. Together. From this day forward.

# *Epilogue*

A week later, the great dining hall of Stanbury Castle was aglow with hundreds of flickering candles, fresh fragrant blossoms and smiling, joyous faces. Dominique was an angelic vision of beauty in a flowing white silk wedding gown, encrusted with millions of seed pearls. Her golden-brown hair was caught up in a cluster of curls and secured beneath multi-layers of filmy white veil.

The dress was the same her mother had worn when she'd wed King Michael thirty-three years before in Edenbourg Abbey. Along with her mother's wedding dress, two days ago Nicholas had presented his younger sister with crown jewels acquired from the Chamber of Riches.

The necklace and earrings were fashioned in a combination of pearls and diamonds set in platinum. The dazzling jewels were a perfect frame for Dominique's beautiful face. Yet their shine couldn't begin to equal the love and happiness glowing in her eyes. Especially

when she looked at her new husband, who'd never yet
left her side since the wedding ceremony three hours
ago at Edenbourg Abbey.

A huge, festive dinner had already been consumed
and the massive tiered wedding cake cut and served.
Waiters were scurrying to and fro with loaded trays of
champagne while at the far end of the room, a sym-
phony ensemble were tuning their instruments in prep-
aration of the wedding ball.

"Even on such short notice, I can't remember the last
time this dining hall was so full of people," Dominique
remarked to Marcus as he finished the last of his second
piece of wedding cake.

He put his empty plate on the table they were standing next to, then curled his arm around the back of
Dominique's waist.

"Edenbourg doesn't have one of their princesses getting married that often," he replied. "The whole country is celebrating."

She smiled up at him. "No one seems to have disapproved of our marriage. Even the tabloids have been
kind, so far."

Marcus chuckled. "That's because none of them
want to face the wrath of the queen."

His comment caused Dominique to gaze across the
room to where her mother was chatting with a longtime
friend of the family. Josephine was dressed in a long
formal gown of deep blue. Her brown hair was fashioned in a smooth, elaborate twist at the back of her
head. Rubies glittered at her ears and throat and wrist.
If King Michael had been at her side, she would have
looked perfect.

"She's been more happy these past few days than

I've seen her since Father's disappearance," Dominique said. "I'm glad we've done that much for her."

Marcus followed his wife's line of vision. "Queen Josephine will be even more happy when you present her with another grandchild."

The thought was consoling to Dominique, yet she wished more than anything that King Michael was here tonight. Especially for her mother's sake. Now that Dominique had Marcus in her life, she understood more than ever how crushed and empty her mother must be feeling without her husband.

"Yes," Dominique agreed. "She will be happy about the baby. But Father's return is what she needs most."

"We all need that," Marcus murmured. "And maybe it will happen soon. Hopefully, long before our baby comes. By the way," he added, "we haven't discussed your plans for after the baby arrives. Are you still going on with plans for the education center?"

Dominique turned in the circle of his arm so that she was gazing up at her husband's handsome face. The past week had passed in a whirlwind and the realization was just now sinking in that she was not just a princess of Edenbourg anymore. She was the wife of the king's high counsel. Her plans would always be centered around him and their marriage.

"Only if you want me to."

He smiled at her generous answer. "Of course I want you to. That's been one of your dreams. It's important that you follow it through."

She was beginning to see that Marcus was going to consider her wishes and desires meaningful to both of them and she had taken a silent vow to always show him how much his thoughtfulness meant to her. She would never take him or his love for granted. Losing her father had taught her how precious was each and every moment of their life together.

"I only need a few more hours to get my degree," she told him. "Hopefully, I can do that with correspondence courses. Or if not, I'll finish my studies here in Edenbourg. I'm not about to go off to New England without you or the baby!"

"I like the sound of that," he whispered. "And maybe, if we're lucky, King Michael will one day see your degree and his new grandchild."

Her eyes shone up at him. "No matter what happens about Father," she said earnestly, "we have each other. And that makes me a very lucky woman already."

Smiling sexily, Marcus lifted a finger to her rosy cheek. "And if you keep looking at me the way you are now, we're going to cut the ball short and slip out of the castle while everyone else is dancing."

Laughing, Dominique slipped her arms around his waist. "What a naughty, delicious thought!"

Across the room, Isabel absently sipped from a champagne glass as she watched her sister and new husband. Their open display of newly found love was a sight for sore eyes and it gladdened her heart to see Dominique so happy. Yet her sister's bliss wasn't the thing that was preoccupying her thoughts at the moment.

Several feet away, Sammy, Jake Stanbury's two-year-old son, was wailing loudly. For the past month, Isabel couldn't help but notice that the boy appeared to be quite a handful for her American cousin. At the moment, he was having little success in pacifying the child, much less keeping him in his seat. Obviously Sammy wasn't accustomed to such social affairs. Nor had he been taught how to behave in public, much less in the presence of a royal family. But then, Jake and his father and brother had never taken part in Edenbourg royalty, she mused. Not until the morning King Michael had disappeared.

In the chair next to Isabel, Rowena, her lady-in-waiting, exclaimed in a low voice, "The poor little tot. He's in misery. Doesn't his father realize this isn't the place for a two-year-old child?"

Isabel glanced thoughtfully at Rowena. "I'm not even sure why Jake or his father and brother are continuing to stay here at the castle." She glanced once again at the dark-haired man who'd supposedly driven up on her father's accident just moments after it had happened. "But I think I know a way to find out," she added with sudden insight.

Twisting around in her chair, Isabel bent her head and said close to Rowena's ear, "I want you to become Sammy's nanny. That way you'll be inside Jake's apartment. You'll be privy to all that goes on between him and Edward and Luke. If any of the three let anything slip about Father's accident, you'll be there to hear it."

Shocked, Rowena stared at her. "Nanny! A spy! Isabel, I can't do it!"

"You must," she said firmly, then before Rowena could make any further protest, she grabbed her by the elbow and tugged her up from the chair. As they began to walk toward Jake, Isabel instructed under her breath, "All I want you to do right now is make Sammy happy and leave the rest to me."

The moment the two women approached Jake he looked up at them with helpless frustration.

"I'm sorry Sammy is causing such a commotion," he apologized. "He wants more cake and I refused because he's already had too much sugar tonight. My son doesn't like the word *no*.''

''Most men don't,'' Rowena replied coolly, then inclined her head toward Sammy, who was still bucking and straining against his father's hold. ''May I take him?''

''Gladly,'' Jake told her.

The instant Rowena lifted him into her arms, the boy quieted. She smiled at him gently and tapped her finger playfully against his little chin.

''You don't really want more cake, do you, young Sammy? You're just tired of sitting in that stiff old chair for so long.''

Sammy nodded in full agreement and wrapped his arms trustingly around Rowena's neck.

Jake rolled his eyes with disbelief. ''Wouldn't you know he'd make a liar out of me,'' he exclaimed. '''More cake' was all I could hear out of the kid.''

''Jake,'' Isabel inserted with a display of sudden excitement, ''have you thought about acquiring a nanny for Sammy? A woman's touch with the boy would surely be a help to the both of you.''

Jake frowned at his cousin's suggestion. ''I wouldn't know where to begin to find a nanny. And even if I did, the poor woman would probably run off screaming after one day of Sammy's tantrums.''

Isabel gestured toward his son. Sammy's tears had dried. He was already talking and making fast friends with Rowena.

''As you can see, Rowena is wonderful with children. If she was in charge of the boy, Sammy wouldn't be having so many tantrums.''

Jake glanced skeptically at Rowena. ''She seems to have him behaving at the moment,'' he cautiously agreed. "But Rowena is your lady-in-waiting, not a nanny."

Isabel dismissed his words with a wave of her hand. "I'm willing to lend her to you. In fact, she's been telling me she doesn't have nearly enough to do, haven't you, Rowena?"

Rowena glanced from her princess to Jake then back to Isabel once again. "That's true. I bore easily if I don't keep busy."

"And you'd be glad to be Sammy's nanny for a while, wouldn't you?" Isabel persisted.

Careful to keep her gaze averted from Jake, Rowena nodded. "Anything to please my princess. And to make a better young man out of Sammy."

Isabel turned a satisfied smile on her American cousin. "See. I've just handed you a perfect nanny. Your troubles are over."

Jake took another long look at the young woman holding his son and decided his generous cousin was wrong. His troubles were just beginning.

\* \* \* \* \*

*Turn the page for a sneak preview of
the next* ROYALLY WED *title,*

## THE BLACKSHEEP PRINCE'S BRIDE

*Jake and Rowena's story!
By rising star Martha Shields
on sale in April 2001
from Silhouette Romance...*

*And don't miss any of the books in
the* ROYALLY WED *series,
only from Silhouette Romance:*

**THE EXPECTANT PRINCESS,**
*March 2001
by Stella Bagwell*

**THE BLACKSHEEP PRINCE'S BRIDE,**
*April 2001
by Martha Shields*

**CODE NAME: PRINCE,**
*May 2001
by Valerie Parv*

**AN OFFICER AND A PRINCESS,**
*June 2001
by Carla Cassidy*

# Chapter One

Rowena Wilde hated this house.

The Dowager Cottage was a dismal place. Built three centuries ago of native granite, the three-story "cottage" sat on the edge of the cliff like an old woman hunkered down against the storms blowing off the North Sea.

It was where extraneous queens grieved for lost husbands, relived former glory, and waited to die.

As she stood with one hand wrapped around a cold iron spoke on the front gate, Rowena recalled the times she'd accompanied Princess Isabel as she visited her grandmother, who'd died three years ago. They would sip tea in the gloomy parlor with heavy velvet curtains shutting out the light. Though central heat had been installed years ago, the house was never warm. Even with a blazing fire. Even in the middle of July.

Rowena had known she'd have to stay here when she and Isabel had concocted this plan. Which was one reason she'd been half hoping Jake Stanbury would refuse to accept her as his son's nanny.

The cottage was full of ghosts, and Rowena had never been comfortable around ghosts.

The other reason, of course, was Jake.

Jake and the Dowager Cottage. Alone, each was a daunting prospect. Together...

Rowena shivered despite the bright afternoon sunlight.

Both Jake and the cottage got her blood pumping, but for vastly different reasons—all related to fear.

Which was ridiculous.

Taking a deep breath, Rowena marshaled her inner resolve.

There was nothing to be afraid of. The cottage was just a pile of stone. She could dissipate the gloom by tearing down the curtains and turning on lamps. And Jake...

Well, she was here for a reason. As long as she kept her mind on her purpose, she wouldn't get sidetracked by feelings she understood all too well...and dreaded.

Rowena forced her lips into her customary smile. Her mother had always said that the best way to conquer fear was to smile your way through it. She'd learned a long time ago that her mother was right. As long as she was smiling, she couldn't scream.

Rowena released the gate latch, wishing she didn't feel like Sleeping Beauty about to prick her finger.


"I'm going to get you."

Jake Stanbury stopped dead, his hand still on the knob of the massive, intricately carved front door. He recognized the voice immediately.

So Rowena Wilde had moved in.

The new nanny's heavily sinister tone seemed to prove the possibility that occurred to him when his royal cousin, Princess Isabel, had suggested her lady-in-waiting as caregiver for his two-year-old son—the possibility that Rowena had been placed in his household as a spy.

What the hell was he going to do now? Leave her here to roam this dreary old house he'd been assigned, poking through his papers? What if she rifled through his things while Sammy was around? Would she blithely tell the boy that his father was suspected of kidnapping the King of Edenbourg?

"I'll find you, Sammy-Jammy. You just wait."

Muffled giggling followed her words.

Relief flooded through Jake. They were playing a game.

Shaking his head, he closed the door and placed his briefcase on the chest in the foyer.

This is what the strain of the past month had brought him to—suspecting a sweet, beautiful young woman of playing Mata Hari. Probably the biggest intrigue Rowena had been involved in was finding the laundress responsible for scorching the princess's favorite gown.

Jake stripped off his suit coat and laid it across his briefcase, then followed the happy sounds to the door of the formal "parlor."

Rowena stood in the middle of the large, over-decorated room, blindfolded, her arms outstretched. His son peeked out from under the coffee table on the other side of the couch, one hand over his mouth to stem the tide of his laughter.

The sight of Sammy having such a good time relieved Jake of any lingering suspicions. Sammy's happiness was all that mattered.

Sammy's giggling should've led Rowena right to him, of course, but she flailed around comically, running into tables and upsetting lamps and antique knickknacks that she pretended to barely catch in time. Her antics sent Sammy into fresh peals of laughter.

Jake couldn't suppress a smile, though the tenderness melting his heart was all for his son.

It definitely wasn't for the petite, auburn-haired beauty bungling around his living room.

The only thing he felt for Rowena was gratitude. He finally had someone he could trust to leave Sammy with. Someone who'd already proved she could coax his son out of his panic attacks and shyness.

Jake leaned against the doorjamb to watch their antics, but straightened abruptly a moment later. Something was out of place. The only item in the room made during the last century was a shiny steel step stool…directly in Rowena's path.

He didn't have time to wonder what it was doing there. Vaulting over the couch, he launched himself off the coffee table just in time to catch Rowena as she stumbled into it.

Their combined momentum took them down, but Jake grabbed her waist and twisted so his back hit the floor first, taking her slight weight.

Rowena didn't scream as they fell, just emitted a quick, "Oh!"

She landed flat on top of him, her legs straddling one of his, her nose buried in his chest. "What in the…?"

Because of the antique Oriental rug covering the centuries old oak floor, Jake wasn't in enough pain to keep his body from reacting—especially when Rowena started squirming to free her hands.

Though his mind denied his feelings every chance it

got, his body knew that he'd been attracted to the curvaceous beauty since the first instant he'd seen her. And now his body reminded his mind of every moment he'd indulged in sensuous fantasies about what his body wanted to do to her body.

He couldn't remember having such a strong reaction to a woman. Ever.

# Don't miss the reprisal of
# Silhouette Romance's popular miniseries

**When
King Michael of
Edenbourg goes
missing,**

*Royally Wed*
*The Stanbury Crown*

his devoted
family and loyal
subjects make it
their mission to bring
him home safely!

## Their search begins March 2001 and continues through June 2001.

On sale March 2001: **THE EXPECTANT PRINCESS**
by bestselling author **Stella Bagwell** (SR #1504)

On sale April 2001: **THE BLACKSHEEP PRINCE'S BRIDE**
by rising star **Martha Shields** (SR #1510)

On sale May 2001: **CODE NAME: PRINCE**
by popular author **Valerie Parv** (SR #1516)

On sale June 2001: **AN OFFICER AND A PRINCESS**
by award-winning author **Carla Cassidy** (SR #1522)

*Available at your favorite retail outlet.*

*Silhouette*®
*Where love comes alive*™

# Silhouette®

## where love comes alive—online...

## eHARLEQUIN.com

## shop eHarlequin

- ♥ Find all the new Silhouette releases at everyday great discounts.
- ♥ Try before you buy! Read an excerpt from the latest Silhouette novels.
- ♥ Write an online review and share your thoughts with others.

## reading room

- ♥ Read our Internet exclusive daily and weekly online serials, or vote in our interactive novel.
- ♥ Talk to other readers about your favorite novels in our Reading Groups.
- ♥ Take our Choose-a-Book quiz to find the series that matches you!

## authors' alcove

- ♥ Find out interesting tidbits and details about your favorite authors' lives, interests and writing habits.
- ♥ Ever dreamed of being an author? Enter our Writing Round Robin. The Winning Chapter will be published online! Or review our writing guidelines for submitting your novel.

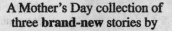
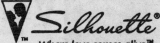

Silhouette
*bestselling authors*

# KASEY MICHAELS

# RUTH LANGAN

# CAROLYN ZANE

*welcome you to a world
of family, privilege and power
with three brand-new love
stories about America's
most beloved dynasty,
the Coltons*

*Brides of Privilege*

Available May 2001

Where love comes alive™